TALES FROM HANS ANDERSEN

FOURTEEN CLASSIC TALES

Selected and illustrated by Edward Ardizzone
Translated by Stephen Corrin

Scholastic Children's Books,
Commonwealth House, 1–19 New Oxford Street, London WC1A 1NU, UK
a division of Scholastic Ltd
London ~ New York ~ Toronto ~ Sydney ~ Auckland
Mexico City ~ New Delhi ~ Hong Kong

First published in hardcover in 1978 by Andre Deutsch Ltd
Revised hardback edition published 1989
First paperback edition published 1989

Translation copyright © Stephen Corrin, 1978
Illustrations copyright © the estate of Edward Ardizzone

ISBN: 0 590 55606 1

Printed and bound by
WSOY, Finland

TALES FROM
HANS ANDERSEN

Montem Primary School
Hornsey Road
London N7 7QT
Tel: 0171 272 6556
Fax: 0171 272 1838

Contents

Translator's Note

In preparing this translation of fourteen tales as a text for Edward Ardizzone's illustrations I have had the assistance of two Danish librarians who were doing a year's stint at the Hendon Library. To Birgitte Ege and Inger Sørensen I owe a debt of gratitude but any shortcomings in the translation are entirely my own.

I have made slight cuts in certain descriptive passages of the longer stories and I may be accused, not without justification, of taking liberties with the original Danish of the master. I have done so only where, to my mind, strict fidelity to the somewhat antiquated language of the text might have made the translation sound oddly bare to the young reader.

The Steadfast Tin Soldier

THERE were once twenty-five tin soldiers, all brothers, because they had all come from one old tin spoon. Muskets on shoulders and very smart in their red and blue uniforms, they all stood there, looking straight ahead. The very first thing they heard when the lid of their box was taken off were the words, "Tin soldiers!" shouted by a little boy clapping his hands. He had been given them as a present and he had arranged them on the table. Each soldier was the spitten image of the other, except for one who was slightly different. He had only one leg, for he had been cast last of all and there hadn't been enough tin left. All the same, he stood just as firm on one leg as the others on their two. And it is precisely this one that our story is about.

On the table where the soldiers stood were many other toys, but the one which immediately caught your eye was a pretty paper castle. Through its tiny windows you could see right into the rooms. Outside it were some little trees arranged round a small looking-glass, which was supposed to look like a lake. Waxen swans were swimming on it and looking at their reflections. It all made a very pretty picture, but the prettiest thing of all was a little lady standing in the open doorway of the castle. She, too, was cut out of paper but she wore a skirt of the most delicate linen and a slim blue strip of ribbon over her shoulder, like a scarf. And in the middle of this ribbon was a gleaming spangle, as big as her whole face. The little lady had both her arms outstretched, for she was a dancer, and one of her legs was raised so high in the air, the tin soldier couldn't see it at all and he thought that she, like him, had only one leg.

"That would be the wife for me," he thought, "but she is very distinguished, she lives in a castle. I have only a box and there are twenty-five of us in it — that's no place for her. Still, I must try to make her acquaintance." Then he lay down full length behind a snuff-box and from there he could see the fine lady, who could remain standing on one leg without losing her balance.

In the evening all the other tin soldiers were placed in the box and the people of the house went to bed. And now the toys began to play. They played at paying visits, making war and giving balls. The tin soldiers rattled in their box, for they wanted to join in, but they couldn't get the lid off. The nut-cracker did somersaults and the slate pencil had great fun with the slate. They all made such a row that the canary woke up and began to talk — and in verse at that. The only two who did not stir from their places were the tin soldier and the little dancer. *She* stood erect on tiptoe with arms outspread, and *he* was just as unbending on his one leg. Not for one second did he take his eyes off her.

And now the clock struck twelve and the snuff-box lid sprang open with a "click". But there was no snuff in it, only a little black troll – it was one of those tricks, a sort of jack-in-the-box.

"Tin soldier," said the troll, "will you keep your eyes to yourself!"

But the tin soldier pretended not to hear.

"Very well, just wait till tomorrow," said the troll.

When the children got up next morning, the little boy placed the tin soldier on the window-sill, and whether it was the troll's mischief or whether there was a sudden draught it is hard to say, but the window suddenly blew open and the tin soldier fell down headlong from the third storey. It was a frightful drop; his leg remained pointed up in the air and he was stuck, with his cap and the point of his bayonet caught between two paving stones. The maid and the little boy went straight down to look for him but though they were as near as anything to treading on him, they couldn't see him. If the tin soldier had only called out, "Here I am!" they would have found him, but he didn't think it proper to call out because he was in uniform.

Then it began to rain. The raindrops fell thick and fast till there was a regular torrent. When it was over, two street boys came by.

"Look!" said one, "there's a tin soldier. Let's sail him." They made a boat out of newspaper, put the tin soldier in the middle and away he sailed down the gutter, with the two lads running alongside, clapping their hands. Heavens above! How high the waves rose and what a current there was! For there had been a real downpour. The paper boat rocked up and down, whirling round and round with such speed that the tin soldier became giddy. But he remained steadfast, looking straight ahead, his musket over his shoulder. Suddenly the boat ducked into a long covered gutter; it was as dark in there as when he had been in his box.

"I wonder where I'm going to now," thought the tin soldier. "This is all the troll's fault! If only the little lady were sitting here

He sailed along the gutter

in the boat, I wouldn't care how dark it was." Just at that moment up came a large water-rat who lived under the covered gutter. "Have you got a pass?" asked the rat. "Show your pass!"

But the tin soldier kept silent and held his musket tighter than ever. The boat sailed on with the rat after it.

Ugh! How the rat gnashed his teeth and shouted to bits of stick and straw as they swept by, "Stop him! He hasn't paid the toll! He hasn't shown his pass!"

But the current got faster and faster. The tin soldier could already see daylight ahead of him, where the gutter came to an end, but he could also hear a roaring noise that might have scared the bravest of men. Just think! Where the covered part of it came to end, the gutter ran straight into a great canal! This, for him, was as frightening as it would be for us to sail down a mighty waterfall! But he was so near, there was no stopping! The boat rushed on, the poor tin soldier held himself as stiff as he could – no one could say of him that he as much as blinked. The boat spun round, three, four times, and filled with water to the very brim. Now it was bound to sink. The tin soldier stood up to his neck in water. Deeper and deeper sank the boat, the paper was falling apart, and now the water closed over the tin soldier's head and he thought of the graceful little dancer whom he would never see again. And in his ears rang the words:

Forward, forward, warrior brave,
For you must suffer death.

The paper boat finally fell apart completely and the tin soldier sank down through it – but at that very instant he was swallowed up by a big fish.

Gracious! How dark it was inside that fish! Even worse than in the covered gutter. And so narrow too. But the tin soldier remained steadfast and lay at full length, his musket over his shoulder. The fish swam all over the place, darting about most alarmingly and then, some time later, it lay quite still, and a ray of light seemed to shoot through it. The light got brighter and a voice cried out, "A tin soldier!" The fish had been caught, taken to market and then brought back into the kitchen, where the maid cut it open with a large knife. She held the soldier with two fingers round his waist and took him into the living-room, where everyone wanted to see the extraordinary man who had travelled round the world in the belly of a fish. But the tin soldier was not in the least bit proud. They stood him on the table and there – it is strange how things happen in this world – there he was in the very room where he had lived before! There were the same children, the same toys on the table. And the beautiful castle with the pretty little dancer! She was still standing on one leg, with the other one high up in the air. She too was steadfast. That touched the tin soldier, he was ready to weep tin tears – but that would not have been proper. He looked at her and she looked at him but they said not a word. Suddenly one of the boys seized the tin soldier and threw him into the stove. He had no reason to do so, it was the troll in the snuff-box who was to blame. The tin soldier lay there, all lit up by the flame, and felt a most overpowering heat. But whether this was due to the real fire or the fire of his love he did not know. All his colours had come off, but nobody could be certain whether this happened during his travels or was due to his sorrow. He looked at the little lady and she looked at him. He felt he was melting but he remained steadfast, his musket over his shoulder. Suddenly the door opened, the wind caught the dancer and she flew like a sylph straight into the stove to the tin soldier. She blazed up and was gone. The tin soldier melted away into a lump and the next morning, when the maid cleared away the ashes, she found him in the shape of a little tin heart. Of the dancer there was nothing left except the spangle, and that was burnt as black as coal.

The Emperor's New Clothes

MANY years ago there was an Emperor who was so madly fond of elegant new clothes that he spent practically all his money trying to look well dressed. He didn't take much interest in his soldiers nor did he bother much about driving into the forest or going to the theatre, unless, of course, it was to show off his smart new clothes. For every hour of the day he had a different suit and if at any time you were to ask where he was, you would be sure to get the reply, "The Emperor is in his dressing-room," and not – as you might expect – "The Emperor is holding a meeting of his councillors."

In the great city where he lived, life was always gay and lively, and the streets were crowded with visitors coming and going. One day two swindlers arrived in the city and told everyone willing to listen that they were weavers who could make the most beautiful cloth imaginable, with the most elaborate patterns and in the richest colours. And they also claimed that the material which they put into the clothes had a most remarkable quality – *it was invisible to anyone who was stupid, or unfit to hold his job.*

"These would indeed be fine clothes!" thought the Emperor. "If I were wearing them I should be able to find out which men in my kingdom were unfit for the posts they held and I could distinguish the fools from the wise. I must have some clothes woven from this material without delay!" And he gave the two swindlers a large sum of money in advance so that they might begin work immediately. They set up two looms and pretended to be weaving, but in reality there was nothing at all on their looms. Then they demanded to be given the finest silk and the costliest gold thread – which they proceeded to put into their own pockets – and worked at the empty looms late into the night.

"I should really like to know how they are getting on with the cloth," thought the Emperor after a couple of days, but the idea that anyone who was stupid or unfit to hold his job would not be able to see it made him feel rather uncomfortable. And though he was confident there was nothing to fear as far as he himself was concerned, he still decided it might be better if he sent someone else along first to see how matters stood. All the people in the city knew what wonderful powers the material possessed and everybody was eager to find out how clever or how stupid his neighbours turned out to be.

"I will send my honest old minister of state to the weavers," thought the Emperor. "He is the best person I know to judge how the stuff looks; he's got good sense and no man is more fit for his post than he is."

So the worthy old minister went along to the hall where the two knaves were sitting and working – or rather pretending to work – at their empty looms. "Heaven preserve us!" thought the old man with a start, opening his eyes very wide. "I can't see anything at all!" But he didn't say a word about it.

The two cheats begged him to be good enough to come closer and asked him whether he did not think the design was most pleasing and the colours beautiful. They pointed to the empty looms and the poor old man stared and stared but he could see nothing, nothing at all, for there was nothing there to see.

"Heaven help me!" he thought. "Am I really so stupid? I have never thought so myself and I certainly am not going to let anyone else think so. Is it possible that I am not fit for my job? No, it would never do for anyone to find out that I could not see the stuff."

"Well, Sir, will you not say whether the material pleases you?" asked one of the weavers.

"Oh, it is most attractive, most charming!" answered the old minister, peering through his spectacles. "What a magnificent pattern and what pleasing colours! Yes, I shall certainly tell the Emperor that I am most pleased with it."

"That is very gratifying!" said the two swindlers, and then they gave names to the shades of colours they had used and described the rare pattern. The old minister listened most attentively for he wanted to repeat it all when he went back to the Emperor. Which is what he did.

And now the two knaves asked for more money and yet more silk and gold thread, which they said they needed for their weaving. They stuffed it all into their own pockets and not a single thread was put on the loom. Then, as before, they went on working at their empty looms.

Shortly after, the Emperor sent another honest official to see how the weavers were getting on with their work and whether the cloth would soon be ready. Exactly the same happened with him as with the old minister. He just stood and stared, but as there wasn't anything at all on the bare looms he couldn't see anything.

"It really is a most beautiful piece of cloth, is it not?" asked the swindlers, pointing out the intricate patterns, and asking him to admire the exquisite colours that weren't there.

"Stupid I most certainly am not," thought the man. "Perhaps I am not fit for my job. It is quite ridiculous, and anyway I must not let it be known." And so he praised the material which he couldn't see and declared his satisfaction with the rich colours and wonderful patterns.

To the Emperor he said: "Yes, the weavers are doing a remarkable job. The cloth is exquisite."

All the people in the city were talking of the magnificent cloth, and at last the Emperor decided he must go and see for himself while the material was still on the loom. Accompanied by a number of specially selected officials, among whom were the two who had already seen it, he went along to the two cunning knaves, who were weaving away for all they were worth without thread or fibre.

"Is not the work truly magnificent?" asked the two officials who had already been there. "Just examine the pattern, Your Majesty, and the exquisite colours." And they pointed to the empty loom, for they thought the others could see.

"What's the meaning of this?" thought the Emperor. "I can't see a thing! This is quite frightening! Am I stupid? Am I not fit to be Emperor? This is the greatest disaster that could happen to me!" But aloud he said, "The cloth is most beautiful. It has Our highest approval." And he kept nodding his head with satisfaction and gazing appreciatively at the empty loom. He would not, he could not, admit that he saw nothing. All the officials who were with him looked and looked but saw nothing, any more than the rest, but, aping their Emperor, they said, "How beautiful it is!" And they advised him to have clothes made from this magnificent material and to wear them for the first time at the great procession which was soon to take place. "Splendid! Magnificent! Exquisite!" were the words on everyone's lips and everybody seemed highly delighted. The

Emperor presented each of the swindlers with the Cross of the Order of Chivalry to wear in his buttonhole and the title of Knight of the Loom.

The whole night long before the morning of the procession the rascals sat up and worked (or rather, pretended to), burning more than sixteen candles, so that people could see that they were hard at work to complete the Emperor's new clothes. They pretended to take the stuff down from the loom; they made cuts in the air with huge scissors; they sewed with needles that had no thread; and finally they said: "Look! The Emperor's clothes are now ready!"

The Emperor came along with his high-born cavaliers and the two knaves raised one arm as though they were holding up something and said, "See, here are the trousers! Here is the coat! Just look at the cloak!" and so on and so forth. "The whole suit is as light as a spider's web. Your Majesty will not feel any weight at all, but that is just the beauty of it."

"Yes indeed!" agreed all the cavaliers; but they couldn't see anything at all for there was nothing to see.

"Would Your Imperial Majesty be graciously pleased to remove your clothes?" asked the knaves. "Then we will fit on the new clothes in front of the great mirror."

The Emperor took off all his clothes and the cheats behaved exactly as though they were fitting him carefully with each garment of his new suit, even pretending to fasten the train, which was to be carried behind him in the procession, round his waist. Then the Emperor turned round and round before the mirror.

"How splendid Your Majesty looks! How beautifully the clothes fit!" they all exclaimed. "What a design! What colours! How truly magnificent is the general effect!"

Then came this announcement from the Chief Master of Ceremonies: "They are waiting outside with the canopy which will be borne above Your Majesty in the procession."

So the Emperor walked in procession under the magnificent canopy

"I am quite ready," said the Emperor. "Does it not fit well?" And once more he turned to the mirror for he wished it to appear as though he were examining his ornate robes with great interest.

The chamberlains, who were to carry the Emperor's train, fumbled about on the ground with their hands as if they were picking up the ends of the mantle; they made as if they were holding something up in the air. They dared not let it be noticed that they could not see anything.

So the Emperor walked in procession under the magnificent canopy and all the people in the streets, as well as those looking out of their windows, said, "How incomparably beautiful are the Emperor's new clothes!" "What a magnificent train he has to his mantle!" "How perfectly it all matches!" No one would let on that there was nothing at all to be seen because by doing so they would have shown themselves to be fools or unfit to hold their posts. Never had the Emperor's clothes excited so much admiration!

"But the Emperor hasn't got on anything at all!" cried a little child.

"Good heavens!" exclaimed his father, "Just listen to what

the innocent child is saying!" And then everybody started whispering to one another what the child had said. The whispers grew louder until the whole people said at last, "But he hasn't got anything on!" And the Emperor got the uncomfortable feeling that what they were saying was only too true; but he thought, "All the same, I must carry on with the procession." And he drew himself up and walked proudly on, and the chamberlains held firmly on to the train that wasn't there at all.

The Little Mermaid

F AR out in the sea the water is as blue as the petals of the most beautiful cornflower and as clear as the purest glass, but it is very deep, beyond the reach of any anchor. Many church towers would have to be placed one on top of the other from the bottom upward to be seen above the water. And deep down below is where the sea-folk live.

Now you must not think that on the bed of the ocean there is only bare white sand. No, the most fantastic trees and plants grow there, with stems and leaves so supple that they respond to the slightest movement of the water, as if they were alive. All the fish, great and small, glide in and out among the branches, just as birds do up here in the air. In the very deepest part lies the palace of the sea-king. Its walls are made of coral and the long, pointed windows are of the clearest amber. The roof consists of mussel-shells which open and close as the water plays on them. It is

23

indeed a most beautiful roof for in every shell lie gleaming pearls, any single one of which would be a lustrous ornament in the crown of a queen.

The sea-king had for many years been a widower but his old mother kept house for him. She was a clever woman but proud of her royal rank and that is why she went about with twelve oysters on her tail – other noble personages were permitted only six. On the whole, though, she deserved high praise, particularly because she lavished such love on her grandchildren, the little sea-princesses. They were six lovely children, the youngest being the most beautiful of them all. Her skin was as fair and pure as a rose leaf, her eyes as blue as the deepest lake, but like all the others she had no legs – her body ended in a fish's tail. The whole day long they would play down in the palace, in the immense halls, where live flowers grew out of the walls. The great amber windows were open and the fish would swim in through them, just as in our world swallows fly in when we open the windows. The fish would swim right up to the little princesses, eat out of their hands and let themselves be stroked.

Outside the palace was a big garden filled with flaming red and dark blue trees. Their fruits glowed like gold and there were flowers, too, that looked like blazing fires because their stems and leaves were never still. The earth itself was of the finest sand but blue like the flame of sulphur. Over it all hung a marvellous blue haze, so that one could more readily believe that one was high up in the air, with the blue sky both above and below, than at the bottom of the sea. When the sea was calm, you could see the sun, looking like some crimson flower from whose calyx all light came streaming out.

Each of the little princesses had her own small plot in the gardens, where she could plant as she pleased. One of them made her plot whale-shaped, another thought it better to have it looking like a mermaid, but the youngest made hers quite round like the sun and had flowers that shone red like it. She was a

Beside this statue she planted a rose-red weeping willow

strange child, quiet and thoughtful. While her sisters would adorn their gardens with the curious things they found on stranded ships, she wanted only the rose-red flowers which looked like the sun, and a pretty marble statue – the statue of a beautiful boy carved out of clear white stone, which had sunk to the sea bed from a wreck. Beside this statue she planted a rose-red weeping willow and it grew splendidly, hanging its verdant branches over the statue down towards the sand-soil where the shadows were violet and, when in movement, imitated the boughs of the trees. It was as if the tree tops and roots were playfully kissing.

There was no greater pleasure for her than to listen to stories about the world of humans up above. Her old grandmother had to tell her all she knew about ships and towns and men and animals. Especially delightful it seemed to her that up there on the earth the flowers were fragrant (for at the bottom of the sea they had no scent) and that the woods were green and that the fish which were to be seen among the branches could sing so charmingly that it was a pleasure to listen to them. What her grandmother called fish were really little birds – because the princess would not have understood what she meant by "birds", never having seen any.

"When you reach the age of fifteen years," said her grandmother, "you will be permitted to swim up to the surface of the sea, to sit on the rocks in the moonlight and watch the great ships sailing by. And you will also see forests and cities."

The next year the eldest sister had her fifteenth birthday. As for the others, each was one year younger than the next, so that the youngest would have to wait five whole years before she dared to swim up from the sea bottom to see how things look in our world. But each sister promised the next to describe all the beautiful things she had found and seen on the first day. For their grandmother didn't really tell them enough and there was such a lot they wanted to know.

26

None of them was as full of yearning as the youngest – and she was precisely the one who had to wait such a long time and who was always so silent and thoughtful. Many a night she would stand by the open window and look up through the dark blue water where the fish beat with their fins and tails. She could see the moon and the stars and though, of course, they shone but faintly they looked much bigger through the water than they seem to our eyes. When something like a black cloud would come floating among them, she knew it was either a whale swimming above her or a ship carrying many people. I don't suppose they ever imagined that a sweet little mermaid stood below them stretching her white arms up towards the keel.

And now the eldest princess attained her fifteenth year and was allowed to swim up above the surface of the sea. When she came back she had hundreds of things to tell, but the most beautiful thing of all, she said, was to lie by moonlight on a sandbank in the calm sea and watch the big city on the sea-shore where, like hundreds of stars, the lights gleamed and twinkled; and to hear the music and the noise and the bustle of carriages and people; and to see the many church steeples and spires and hear the bells ringing.

And precisely because she was not allowed to go up there, the youngest sister yearned for it all the more ardently. Oh! How she did listen! And when, late in the evening, she stood by the open window and looked up through the dark blue water, she thought about the big city with all its noise and bustle and she imagined she could hear the church bells ringing down to her.

The following year the second sister got leave to swim up and go wherever she pleased. Up she went just as the sun was going down, and the sight of this was, she thought, the most beautiful sight of all. The whole sky had looked like gold, she said, and she couldn't even begin to describe the beauty of the clouds: red and violet, they had sailed above her, but even swifter than the clouds, like a long white veil, flew a flock of wild swans – away over the water where the sun was setting. She had swum towards it but it sank and the rose tints faded from the clouds and the surface of the sea.

The following year the third sister went up. She was the most daring of them all. She swam up and then inland into a wide river which flowed into the sea. She espied beautiful green hills clothed with rows of vines; castles and forts peeped out from magnificent woods. She heard all the birds singing and the sun was so hot that from time to time she had to dive under the water to cool her burning face. In a little bay she came upon a crowd of small men-children, quite naked, running around and splashing about in the water. But when she wanted to play with them, they ran away. And then a little black animal appeared (it was a dog but she had never seen one before) which barked at her so furiously that she was terrified and escaped into the open sea. But she could not forget those splendid woods, the green hills and the pretty children, who could swim in the water even though they had no fishtails.

The fourth sister was not so bold. She kept to the open sea and told them there wasn't anything more beautiful than that. You could see for many miles around and the sky above was like an enormous glass bell. She had seen ships, but from afar they looked like sea-gulls. The dolphins were funny and had turned somersaults around her. The huge whales had squirted jets of water from their nostrils, just like hundreds of fountains.

Now it was the fifth sister's turn. Her birthday fell in winter and so she was able to see what the other sisters hadn't seen when they first swam up. The sea looked quite green and all around there were great icebergs, each one resembling a pearl, and yet they were much bigger than the church towers that man had built. They were of the most curious shapes and they sparkled like diamonds. She had sat down on one of the largest and all the sailing vessels, in alarm, had kept themselves as far away as possible from where she was sitting, letting the wind blow her long hair about. But towards evening the sky became overcast; there was thunder and lightning, while the black sea lifted the great blocks of ice high up, making them glow in the flashes of lightning. On all the ships they had taken down the sails and there was fear and dread in every heart, but she had sat quietly on her floating iceberg, watching the flashes as they zigzagged into the glistening sea.

The first time the sisters had come up to the surface of the water, they had each been thrilled by everything new and beautiful there was to be seen. But now that they were grown up and were allowed to swim up whenever they wished, these things had no further interest for them and they longed to get back home again. After being away for a month or two they decided that everything was much more beautiful down below and, in any case, it was so pleasant to be in one's own home.

Many an evening the five sisters would link arms and rise to the surface together. They had sweet voices, more beautiful than the voice of any human being, and whenever a storm was blowing up and they were afraid that some ships might get lost,

they would swim in front of them and describe in their song how beautiful it was at the bottom of the sea and tell the sailors not to be afraid of coming down. But the men on board the ships could not understand the words – they thought it was the noise of the storm. Nor was there anything beautiful down there for them to see, for when the ship sank the men drowned and if they ever reached the sea-king's palace it was only as corpses.

When the sisters came up like this, arm-in-arm, through the sea, the little sister stayed behind all alone, following them with her eyes; and it was as if she had to cry, but a mermaid does not have tears and so her suffering is all the greater.

"Oh! If I were only fifteen!" she cried. "I know I shall grow really fond of the world up there and of the people who build and live there."

At last she was fifteen years old. "Well now, we have got you off our hands," said her grandmother, the old widow queen. "Come and let me adorn you as I did your sisters." And she set a garland of white lilies on her hair. Each petal in the flower was a half-pearl, and the old queen had eight big oysters grip the princess's tail fast to mark her high rank.

"It is very painful," said the princess.

"Yes," said the old queen, "but one has to bear pain for the sake of one's station."

Oh! How she would gladly have shaken off all her fine adornments and laid aside the heavy garland (the red flowers from her garden looked much better on her), but she did not dare do so.

"Goodbye!" she said and then she rose up, bright and clear as an air-bubble, through the water.

The sun had only just set when she raised her head above the waves, but all the clouds glowed rose and golden and in the midst of the pale red haze the evening star gleamed clear and bright. The air was soft and fresh and the sea perfectly calm. A great three-masted ship lay close by but only one sail was unfurled, for there was not a breath of wind. And sailors were sitting all about, in the rigging or on the topmast. There was music and singing and as the evening got darker hundreds of parti-coloured lamps were lit. It was as if the flags of all the nations were hanging in the wind. The little mermaid swam right up to the cabin window and each time she rose upon the waves she could see through the clear porthole glass lots of smartly dressed men. The most handsome of all was the young prince with the great dark eyes. He could not be much more than sixteen years old; this was his birthday and that was why everything was so festive. The sailors were dancing on the deck and when the young prince appeared, hundreds of rockets whizzed up into the sky, with a light brighter than the light of day. The little mermaid was quite scared and dived beneath the water, but she soon rose up again and it was as though all the stars were falling from the sky down upon her. Never had she seen such fireworks. Huge suns hummed and whirred around her, fiery fish darted up into the blue air and everything was reflected back from the clear calm sea. It was so light on the ship itself that even the smallest rope was visible, and the men clearest of all. How handsome the young prince looked! He was shaking hands with people, smiling and laughing, while the music rang out in the glorious night.

It was getting late but the little mermaid could not take her eyes away from the ship and the handsome prince. The coloured lanterns were now put out, there were no more rockets in the air, nor was there any further boom of guns, but deep down in the sea there was a murmuring and rumbling. Meanwhile the mermaid sat on the water, rocking up and down, so that she could see into the cabin. The ship now moved at a faster pace, one sail after another was unfurled, the waves grew stronger, great clouds gathered in the sky and there were flashes of lightning in the distance. A wild and frightening storm was brewing and the sailors took down the sails. The great ship tossed over the wild waters as it flew forward, the waves rose up like huge black mountains as though they wanted to overturn the masts, but the ship plunged down like a swan in the midst of the massive waves and rose aloft once again as the breakers came crashing down. The little mermaid took it all to be nothing more than a rather boisterous passage but to the seamen it seemed very different indeed! The ship groaned and creaked, the stout timbers shivered as the billowing sea crashed against the ship; the main mast snapped as though it were no stronger than a reed and the ship lurched heavily on her side as the water streamed into her hold. Now the little mermaid could see they were in danger and she herself had to beware of the beams and fragments of the ship as they were flung into the water. One moment everything became so coal-black that she couldn't see anything at all and then, when the lightning flashed, it became so bright she could make out every man on board. Each one was staggering about as best as he could. She sought out the young prince and caught sight of him as the ship broke in pieces and sank into the deep. Just for a split second she was filled with happiness, for now he would be coming down to her, but then she remembered that men cannot live in the water and that the prince could never come down to her father's palace unless he were dead. No! He must not die! She swam about among the drifting beams and planks, forgetting that she herself might be crushed by them, plunged deep down and then rose again among the waves till she reached the young prince, who was barely able to swim any longer in the turbulent waves. His arms and legs were losing their strength, his beautiful eyes were closed and he surely would have died had not the little mermaid come to him. She held his head above the water and let the waves carry her with him wherever they would.

By the next morning the storm had abated. There was not a fragment of the ship to be seen. The sun came up red and glowing from the waves and it seemed that with it life came into

the prince's cheeks, though his eyes remained closed. The little mermaid kissed his noble brow and stroked his wet hair. She thought he looked like the marble statue in her little garden. She kissed him again and wished ardently that he might live. And now in front of her she saw firm land and lofty blue hills on whose peaks the snow shone as if swans had settled on them. Down near the shore there were pleasant green woods and in front of them was a building of some sort – a church or monastery (she did not know). Lemon and apple trees grew in the garden and by the gate were tall palm trees. The sea had formed a little bay here, and right up to the rocks where the fine white sand was washed up, the sea, though calm, was very deep. And here the little mermaid swam with the handsome prince and laid him on the sand, taking great care that his head should face the warm sun. And now bells began to ring through the big white building and several young girls came out through the garden. The little mermaid swam further out behind some high rocks which rose above the waves. She hid her hair and breast with the sea-foam so that no one might see her and then she waited for someone to come and help the poor prince.

It was not long before a young girl came by. She seemed frightened at first but only for a few seconds, then she went and fetched some more people, and the mermaid saw the prince come to life again and smile to all those around him. But he had no smile for her out there; nor, of course, could he know that she had rescued him. The little mermaid's heart sank, and when he had been taken into the big building she plunged sadly down into the water and returned home to her father's palace.

She had always been silent and thoughtful but now she became even more so. Her sisters asked her what she had seen on her first visit to the earth but she told them nothing.

Many an evening and morning she would go up to the place where she had left the prince. She watched the fruits in the garden grow ripe and saw them being plucked. She saw the snow melt from the high mountains, but the prince she never saw, and so she always returned to her home even sadder than before. Her one consolation was to sit in her little garden and fling her arms around the beautiful marble statue which resembled the prince, but she neglected her flowers and they grew, as in a wilderness, over all the paths and interlaced their long stems and leaves with the branches of the trees, so that the place became quite dark.

At last she could bear it no longer and told one of her sisters her story. Almost immediately all the other sisters got to know – but nobody else except a couple of mermaids who told only their closest friends. One of these had found out who the prince was and she had also seen the merrymaking on board his ship and she knew where he came from and where his kingdom lay.

"Come, little sister," said the other princesses, and with their arms around each others' shoulders they rose up in a line out of the sea to the place where they knew the prince's palace lay.

The palace was built of pale yellow gleaming stonework, with great marble steps, down which one went straight to the sea. Magnificent golden cupolas rose above the roof, and between the colonnades which surrounded the entire building there were marble images that seemed almost alive. Through the clear glass of the high windows one could see into the stately halls with their precious hangings and tapestries; and all the walls were adorned with great paintings which were a delight to look at. In the centre of the largest hall there was a great fountain whose waters soared up into the glass cupola in the ceiling and through which the sun shone on the water and on the beautiful plants that grew in the wide basin.

So now she knew where the prince lived and it was there that she went many an evening and night. She would swim much closer to the land than any of her sisters had ventured to. She even dared to swim up to the small canal beneath the splendid marble balcony which cast a long shadow over the water, and here she would sit and gaze upon the young prince, who believed he was all alone in the bright moonlight. Many a time she saw him sailing in his magnificent boat with its banners flying while the music played. She would peep out from behind the green sedge, and if the breeze rippled her long silver veil and anyone happened to see it, they took it to be a swan spreading its wings. Many a night when the fishermen were out at sea with their torches, she heard them saying good things about the prince and this pleased her, for she had rescued him when he was drifting half-dead on the waves. And she remembered how firmly his head had rested on her breast and how fervently she had kissed him. But he, of course, knew nothing at all of this and it could not even be part of his dreams.

She began to love human beings more and more and longed to live among them. It seemed to her that their world was much bigger than hers: they could race across the sea in ships, climb high mountains above the clouds, and the lands that belonged to them, with their fields and forests, extended farther than the eye could see. There was so much she felt she wanted to know, but her sisters could not answer all her questions so she asked her old

She would peep out from behind the green sedge

grandmother, who knew so much about "that world up there", as she so aptly called the lands above the sea.

"If men do not drown, do they live for ever?" the little mermaid asked her. "Do they not die as we do under the sea?"

"Yes," said the old lady, "they must die, too, and, besides, their lifetime is shorter than ours. We can live for three hundred years but when we have finished living we only become foam on the water – we do not even have a grave down here among our loved ones. We have no immortal souls, we do not live anew when we die, but are like the green sea-sedge – if it is cut away it cannot blossom again. Men, on the other hand, have a soul that lives on, lives always, even after the body has turned to earth. It rises through the air up to the bright stars. Just as we swim up to the surface of the sea to see the land of human beings, so do they rise up to unknown glorious places which we are never to see."

"Why have we no immortal soul?" asked the little mermaid sadly. "I would give up all my hundreds of years that I have before me if I could live as a human being for just one single day and have a share in their heavenly world!"

"You must not think of such things," said the old lady. "We are far happier and better off here than the human beings up there."

"So shall I die then and drift like foam upon the waves?" asked the little mermaid, "and not hear the sound of waves and see the lovely flowers and the red sun? Can I do nothing at all to gain an immortal soul?"

"No," said the old lady, "unless a man were to love you so dearly that you meant more to him than his own mother and father; and unless he were to cling to you with all his mind and heart and let the priest place his right hand in yours with a promise to be true to you here and to all eternity. Then would his soul pass into your body and you too would have a part in man's happiness. He would give you a soul and still keep his own. But that can never happen. The very thing that is considered by us in the sea as beautiful – I mean your fish's tail – they up there on earth find ugly. They don't know any better. They think that in order to be beautiful one must have two unwieldy props, which they call legs."

The little mermaid fetched a deep sigh and looked sadly at her fish's tail. "Let us be contented," said the old lady. "We shall skip and dance for the three hundred years of our lives; that is time enough, to be sure! Then one can rest all the better in one's grave! Tonight we shall give a court ball."

What a magnificent affair it was! The like of it has never been seen on earth. The walls and ceiling of the immense ballroom were of thick but transparent glass. Hundreds upon hundreds of huge mussel-shells, rose-red and grass-green, hung in rows on either side, lit by a blue flame that illuminated the entire hall and shone through the walls, casting its glow on the sea outside. You could see the numberless fish, big and small, swimming against the glass walls, some with scales of crimson and violet, others bright with silver and gold. Through the centre of the hall flowed a rapid stream along which mermaids and mermen danced to the music of their own sweet song. Such beautiful voices are not given to human beings on earth. The little mermaid sang more prettily than anyone and they clapped their hands to applaud her, and for a brief moment she felt a thrill of joy, for she knew that she had the most beautiful voice of anyone on land or on sea. But her thoughts soon turned once more to the world above her. She could not forget the handsome prince, nor her grief that, unlike him, she had no immortal soul. So she stole out of her father's palace and while everything there was song and gaiety she sat all downcast in her little garden. Then she heard the sound of the horn echoing through the water and she thought, "Now, surely, that is he sailing above me, he whom I love more than my father and my mother, he who ever fills my thoughts and in whose hands I would place my life's happiness. To win him and to gain an immortal soul I would risk all.

While my sisters are dancing in my father's palace, I will go to the sea-witch whom I have always dreaded but who, perhaps, can advise and help me."

And so the little mermaid went out of her garden and swam out towards the raging whirlpool beyond which the sea-witch lived. She had never gone that way before. No flowers grew there, no sea-grass, only barren grey sand stretched away towards the pool, where the water, like a raging mill-wheel, whirled round and round and pulled everything it caught hold of down into the deep. Through those whirling waters she had to pass before she could enter the sea-witch's realm, towards which there was no other path except a long stretch of hot bubbling slime which the sea-witch called her peat bog. Behind this lay her house, in the middle of a mysterious forest. All the trees and bushes in it were polypi, half beast and half plant, which looked like hundred-headed serpents growing out of the earth. All the branches were long slimy arms with fingers like supple worms, each joint of which was in ceaseless movement, from the roots to the outermost tip. Everything in the sea that they could get into their clutches they enlaced themselves around, never to let go. The little mermaid paused in deadly terror at the sight of them; her heart beat in panic, and she would have turned back had she not thought of the prince and of man's immortal soul. That restored her courage. She wound her long floating hair tight round her head so that the polypi should not catch it. She placed her hands over her breast and then darted off through the water, as fast as any fish, and in among the ugly polypi, which stretched out their supple arms and fingers to catch her. She could see how every one of them had caught something, how hundreds of little arms held it fast like strong iron bands. Men who had perished at sea and had sunk down into the deep stared like white skeletons from between the arms of the polypi. There were rudders and sea chests clutched tight and skeletons of land animals and, most terrifying of all, a little mermaid, whom they had caught prisoner and strangled. And now she had come to a large swampy clearing in the woods where great fat water-snakes wallowed in the mud, showing their ugly yellowish bellies. In the middle of the clearing stood a house made with the white bones of ship-wrecked men, and there sat the sea-witch, letting a toad eat out of her mouth just as human beings let a canary peck sugar. She called the loathsome fat snakes her little chicks and allowed them to wallow over her large fungus-covered bosom.

"I know what you're after," mocked the sea-witch, "and very foolish of you it is, too. All the same, you shall have your wish for it will bring you misfortune, my charming princess. You would like to be rid of your fish's tail and to have instead two supports to walk on, like human beings, so that the young prince may fall in love with you and so that you may, like him, gain an immortal soul." And saying all this the sea-witch burst into a laugh so loud and foul that the toad and the snakes fell from her to the earth and lay there wallowing in the slime.

"You've come just at the right time," she went on. "Tomorrow, after the sun has risen, I wouldn't be able to help you until another year had passed. I shall prepare you a drink and with it you must swim to the land before sunrise, sit down on the shore there and drink it. Then your fish's tail will separate and contract into what human beings call beautiful legs. But it will be painful, like a sharp sword cutting right through you. Everyone who beholds you will say you are the loveliest human child they have ever seen. You will retain the grace of your swimming movements – no dancer could proceed more gracefully than you – but every *step* you take will be as though you were treading on a sharp knife – so sharp that blood will gush out. Will you suffer all this? If so, I can help you."

"Yes," said the little mermaid, her voice trembling. And she thought about the prince and about gaining an immortal soul.

"But remember," said the witch, "when once you have taken on a human form, you can never again be a mermaid! You will

never again be able to go down to your father's palace or see your sisters. But if you do *not* win the prince's love, so that he thinks *only* of you and forgets his mother and his father and lets the priest clasp your hands in one another's to make you man and wife – then you will get no immortal soul! And on the very first morning after he is wedded to another, your heart will surely break and you will drift like foam on the waves."

"I will have it so," said the little mermaid, pale as death.

"But you must pay me as well!" continued the witch. "And it is no small thing that I demand. Yours is the most beautiful voice of anyone down here on the sea bed, and with that voice you doubtless believe you can charm your prince – but that voice you must give to me. The finest thing that you possess I must have for my precious potion. I must mix my own blood with it so that the draught becomes as sharp as a two-edged sword."

"But if you take away my voice," said the little mermaid, "what have I got left?"

"Your lovely form, your graceful gait and your eloquent eyes," said the witch. "With those you could lead a human heart astray. Well now, have you lost courage? Put out your little tongue and I shall cut it off in payment and then you will receive the potent draught."

"So let it be," said the little mermaid, and the witch put a cauldron on the fire to brew her devilish mixture.

"Cleanliness is a good thing," she said, scrubbing the cauldron with some snakes which she had tied into a knot. Then she made a gash in her breast and let black blood drip into the cauldron. The steam, as it rose, took on the most horrifying shapes and every moment the witch kept throwing something fresh into the brew. When it came to the boil it made the noise of a crocodile crying. But when finally the potion was ready, it looked like the purest water.

"There you have it," said the witch and cut out the little mermaid's tongue, so that now she was dumb and could neither sing nor speak.

"If the polypi should try and grab hold of you on your way back through my woods," said the witch, "just throw one single drop of this potion at them and their arms and fingers will split into a thousand pieces." But the little mermaid had no need to do this for the polypi drew back in terror when they saw the glittering drink shining in her hand like some twinkling star. And the princess did not take long to get through the woods, the swamp and the raging whirlpool.

She could see her father's palace. The torches were no longer alight in the great ballroom. Everyone inside was no doubt asleep. But she did not dare look for anyone now that she was dumb and would be leaving them for ever. She felt her heart would break from grief. She crept into the garden and took a flower from each of her sister's flower-beds, threw a thousand kisses with her fingers towards the palace and floated up through the dark blue sea.

The sun had not yet risen when she saw the prince's palace and climbed the splendid marble steps. The moon shone bright and clear. She drank down the burning, cutting brew and it felt as though a double-edged sword was penetrating her delicate body; she fainted with pain and lay as one dead. When the sun shone out over the sea she woke up with the sensation of a stinging pain, but there in front of her stood the handsome young prince. He fastened his coal-black eyes upon her and she cast her eyes downwards and saw that her fish's tail was gone and that she now had the prettiest, dainty white legs that any girl could wish to have. But she was quite naked and so she wrapped herself in her long luxuriant hair. The prince asked her who she was and how she had come there. And she, so tenderly and yet so sorrowfully, gazed at him with her dark blue eyes but could not speak. Then he took her by the hand and led her into the palace. Every step she took was, as the witch had warned, as if she were treading on sharply pointed, keen-edged knives, but she endured it gladly. With her hand in the prince's she moved on, light as a soap-bubble, and he, like everybody else, wondered at her graceful, floating walk.

She was arrayed in rich robes of silk and muslin and there was none more beautiful than her in all the palace, but she was dumb and could neither sing nor speak. Lovely slave girls dressed in silks and gold came and sang before the prince and his royal parents. One of them sang more prettily than the others and the prince clapped his hands and smiled at her, and this made the little mermaid very sad for she knew that she herself had once sung far more sweetly. She thought, "Oh! If he only knew that in order to be near him I have sacrificed my voice for ever!" Then the slave girls danced their delightful swaying dance to the sound of the most entrancing music and when they had finished, the little mermaid, her slender arms raised high, glided on tiptoe over the floor in a dance the like of which had never yet been seen. With every movement her beauty grew more striking and her eyes spoke more to the heart than the slave girl's song. Everyone was enchanted, especially the prince, who called her his little foundling. She danced on and on, though every time her feet touched the ground she felt she was treading on sharp knives. The prince said that she must always be with him and she was permitted to sleep on a velvet cushion outside his door. The prince ordered a boy's costume to be made for her so that she might accompany him on horseback when he went out riding. They rode through the fragrant woods where the green branches touched their shoulders and little birds sang from behind the young leaves. She climbed the high hills by the prince's side, and though her tender feet bled for all to see, she laughed and followed him till they saw the clouds beneath them sail away like a flock of birds setting off for distant lands.

At home in the prince's palace, when everybody else was asleep at night, she would go out to the broad marble steps, and cool her burning feet in the cold water; then she would think of the others down there in the deep.

One night her sisters came up arm-in-arm singing their sorrowful song as they swam through the water, and the little mermaid motioned to them and they recognised her and told her how sad she had made them all. From then on they came to see her every night and once she saw, far out to sea, her old grandmother, who for many years had not come up to the surface of the water; and also the sea-king, with his crown on his head. They stretched out their hands towards her but they did not venture as near land as the sisters.

Day by day the prince grew more fond of her, and he loved her as one loves a dear, good child; but the thought of making her his queen never once occurred to him. And yet, she had to become his wife, otherwise she could never win an immortal soul, and on his very wedding-morn she would change into sea-foam.

"Do you not love me more than all the others?" the little mermaid's eyes seemed to ask when he took her in his arms and kissed her beautiful forehead.

From then on they came to see her every night

"Yes, you are the dearest of all to me," the prince would say, "for you have the best heart of them all. You are the most devoted and you are like a young girl whom I once saw but shall, I somehow feel, never find again. I was on a ship that was wrecked and the waves carried me to land close to a sacred temple, where several young maidens served. The youngest found me on the sea-shore and saved my life. I saw her only twice. She was the only one in the whole world whom I could love and you are very like her. You almost take the place of her image in my soul. She belongs to that sacred temple; good fortune has sent you to me – never shall we be parted!"

"Ah! He does not know that I saved his life," thought the little mermaid, "that I carried him over the waves to the woods, where the temple stands; that I sat behind him in the foam, waiting to see whether anyone would come to save him. I was the pretty girl whom he loves more than me!" And the little mermaid sighed deeply – she could not weep. "He says that the girl belongs to the sacred temple. So she will never come out into the world; they can never meet again. But I am with him every day; I will care for him and love him and offer him my life."

But now the prince was to be married to the beautiful daughter of the king of a neighbouring land – so the people said. That was why he was equipping such a splendid ship. It was also being said, of course, that the prince was making his voyage in order to see the neighbouring country, but it was really to see the neighbouring king's daughter. And he was to have a great retinue of courtiers to accompany him. But the little mermaid shook her head and laughed, for she knew the prince's thoughts better than anyone.

"I must make the voyage," he had told her. "I must see the beautiful princess, my parents desire me to do so; but they cannot compel me to bring her back home as my bride. I cannot love her, she does not resemble the beautiful girl in the temple, as you do. If ever I choose a bride, I should choose you first, my silent foundling with the eloquent eyes!" And he had kissed her rosy mouth, played with her long hair and laid his head upon her heart. And she dreamed of human happiness and an immortal soul.

"You have no fear of the sea, my silent child?" the prince asked her as they stood on the fine ship bearing them away to the country of the neighbouring king. And he spoke to her of storms and of calm sea, of rare fish down in the deep and of what divers had seen down there. And she smiled at his tales for she, better than anyone else, knew what went on at the bottom of the sea.

In the moonlit night when everyone except the helmsman at the wheel was asleep, she sat on the ship's side and stared down through the clear water, and she thought she saw her father's palace. On the topmost part stood her old grandmother with a silver crown on her head, staring up through the rapid current at the ship's keel. Then her sisters came up above the water, staring sorrowfully at her and wringing their hands. She beckoned to them and smiled. She wanted to tell them that everything was going well with her, but just then the cabin boy came by and the sisters dived down – so he fancied that the patch of white he had seen was the foam on the waves.

Next morning the ship sailed into the harbour of the neighbouring king's splendid city. All the church bells were ringing and from the lofty towers came the sound of trumpets, while soldiers stood with banners flying and bayonets glittering. Everybody was on holiday. Balls and celebrations succeeded one another, but meanwhile the princess had not yet appeared. She was being instructed in a sacred temple far away from there, they said, and there she was learning all the royal virtues. At last she arrived. The little mermaid stood waiting, eager to see her beauty, and she had to acknowledge that never had she seen a more graceful figure. Her skin was clear and delicate and from beneath the long dark eyelashes smiled a pair of innocent deep blue eyes.

"It is you!" exclaimed the prince. "You who saved me when I lay lifeless on the shore!" And he clasped the blushing bride in his arms. "Oh, I am so very happy!" he said to the little mermaid. "The most that I ever dared to hope has come true for me! You will rejoice in my happiness for you have loved me most of all." And the little mermaid kissed his hand and thought her heart would break. On his wedding-morn she would die and change into foam upon the waves.

All the church bells were ringing. Heralds rode through the streets and announced the betrothal. On the altars in the churches perfumed oil burned in costly silver lamps. The priests swung their censers and the bride and bridegroom held each other's hand and received the bishop's benediction. The little mermaid, dressed in silk and gold, held up the bride's train but her ears did not hear the festive music, her eyes did not see the sacred ceremony. She was thinking of the night which would precede her death and of everything she had lost.

That same evening the bride and bridegroom went on board ship. Cannons were fired and banners waved, and in the middle of the main deck a magnificent tent of purple and gold with the softest of cushions was set up, in which the bridal pair were to sleep on that calm, cool night.

The sails swelled in the wind and the ship glided easily and smoothly over the clear waters. When it grew dark, gaily coloured lamps were lit and the sailors danced jolly dances on deck. The thoughts of the little mermaid turned to that first time, when she rose up above the water and beheld that same gaiety and splendour. She remembered how she had whirled around among the other dancers, soaring as a swallow does in the air when it is being pursued; how everyone had cheered her in wonder, for never had they seen anyone dance so brilliantly. She felt the sharp knives cutting her delicate feet but in her heart the pain was much keener. She knew this was the last time she would see him – him for whose sake she had abandoned her family and her home, had sacrificed her lovely voice and daily endured ceaseless pain. Nothing of all this had ever crossed his mind! This was to be the last night she would breathe the same air as he, look upon the deep sea and the starry heavens. An everlasting night, without thoughts or dreams, awaited her, for she had no soul nor could she gain one.

On board ship till long after midnight all was joy and gaiety; and she laughed and danced with the thought of death heavy on her heart. The prince kissed his lovely bride and she played with his dark hair, and, arm-in-arm they went to rest in the magnificent tent.

On the ship all was silent and still; there was only the helmsman standing at the wheel. The little mermaid laid her white arms on the bulwarks and looked towards the east for the first pink of dawn: the first rays of the sun, she knew, would be her death. Then she saw her sisters rising up out of the water. Pale they were, as she was, and their long lustrous hair no longer fluttered in the wind, it had been cut off.

"We have given it to the witch so that she might help us to save your life, so that you may not die this night. She has given us a knife. Here it is. See how sharp it is! Before the sun rises you must plunge it into the prince's heart and when his warm blood drops to your feet they will grow together again into a fish's tail and you will be a mermaid again and you can come down to us and live your three hundred years before you change into salt foam on the sea. Hurry! Either he or you must die before sunrise. Our old grandmother is mourning, her white hair is falling off, just as ours fell before the witch's scissors. Kill the prince and come back to us! Hurry! Do you not see the red streak in the sky? In a few moments the sun will rise into the heavens and then you must die!" And with a strange, deep sigh they vanished beneath the waves.

The little mermaid pulled aside the purple hanging of the tent and saw the beautiful bride asleep, her head resting on the

prince's breast. She bowed and kissed his handsome brow, looked up at the sky where the red light of dawn shone ever brighter, gazed at the sharp knife and once more fastened her eyes on the prince, who, in his sleep, was calling his new bride by name; she alone filled his thoughts. The knife trembled in the little mermaid's hand ... and then she flung it far out on to the waves, which glowed red where it fell. It was as if red drops of blood gushed up from the sea. Yet once again, her eyes half glazed, she looked at the prince, flung herself from the ship and felt her body dissolve into foam.

Now the sun came up from the sea and its rays fell so warm and bright on the dead-cold foam that the little mermaid did not feel the hand of death. She could see the bright sun and, hovering above her, hundreds of beautiful transparent forms, through which she could glimpse the white sails of the ship and the pink clouds in the heavens. Their voices were music, but so heavenly that no human ears could hear them, just as no earthly eye could see them. Without wings, they floated through the air, kept aloft by their very lightness. The little mermaid saw that she had a body like theirs and she felt herself gradually rising from the foam.

"To whom am I coming?" she asked, and her voice sounded like that of the other beings, so heavenly that no earthly music can render it.

"To the daughters of the air!" replied the others. "A mermaid has no immortal soul and she can never gain one unless she wins the love of a mortal being. Her eternal existence lies with a power that is not hers. The daughters of the air have no immortal soul but they can win one by their own good deeds. We are flying to warmer lands where the fetid air of pestilence strikes men down and there we bring coolness. We spread the fragrance of flowers through the air to restore men to health and vigour. When we have striven for three hundred years to do all the good we can, we receive an immortal soul and a share in man's eternal happiness. You, poor little mermaid, with all your heart, have sought the same thing. You have suffered and borne pain and raised yourself into the world of the beings of the air. And now, you can yourself, by good deeds, after three hundred years, acquire an immortal soul." The little mermaid raised her slender arms towards God's sun and for the first time she felt tears. On board ship there was once more bustle and movement. She saw the prince and his lovely bride looking for her, staring sorrowfully down at the billowing foam, as if they knew that she had thrown herself to the waves. Invisible, she kissed the bride's brow, smiled at the prince and, with the other children of the air, rose up towards the pink clouds sailing through the heavens.

"In three hundred years' time we shall soar into God's kingdom."

"Even sooner," whispered one of them. "Unseen we enter the

houses of men where there are children; and every day that we see a good child, who makes its parents happy and earns their love, God takes away from our time of probation. The child does not know of this as we pass through his room, but as we smile joyfully at him one whole year is taken off the three hundred! But if we see a naughty, ill-natured child, we must weep tears of sorrow, and every tear adds one more day to our time of trial!"

The Flying Trunk

THERE was once a merchant who was so rich he could have paved a whole street – and perhaps a little alley as well – with silver coins. But he didn't do that. He knew other ways of spending his money: before he spent *one* shilling, he made sure he could get *twenty* back. That's the sort of merchant he was! And he went on like that – until, finally, he died.

All his money went to his son, who had a high old time. He went to a fancy-dress ball every night, made paper kites out of bank-notes and played ducks and drakes on the lake with *gold sovereigns* instead of with stones. I daresay that's a quick way of getting rid of your money, and that is exactly what happened. In the end he had only four shillings left and no clothes apart from a pair of old slippers and a dressing-gown. His friends no longer cared about him and wouldn't even be seen in the street with him – that is, all of them except one, who was kind and who sent him an old trunk and told him to "Pack up!" Well, a fat lot of good that was, for he had nothing to pack; so he got into the trunk himself.

It was an odd sort of trunk: as soon as you pressed the lock, it would fly! And that is what it did! Up it flew, with the young man in it, through the chimney, high up above the clouds and far, far away. The bottom of the trunk kept creaking and he was scared it might break to pieces, and if it had, he would have had to make quite a jump, Heaven preserve us! But at last he reached the land of the Turks. He hid the trunk in some woods under a pile of withered leaves and went into the town – where he found he could mix quite easily, for the Turks all went about dressed like him, in dressing-gown and slippers. In the street he met a nurse with a small child.

"Listen here, you Turkish nurse," he said to her, "what's that great big castle just outside the town with the windows set so high up in the walls?"

"That's where the king's daughter lives," replied the nurse. "It's been said that when she falls in love her lover will make her unhappy, and so nobody may visit her unless the king and queen are there with her."

"Thank you," said the merchant's son, and he went back into the wood, got into his trunk, flew up on to the roof of the castle and crept in at the window to the princess.

She was lying asleep on the sofa and she looked so pretty that the merchant's son had to kiss her. She woke up and was terribly frightened. But he told her he was a Turkish god who had especially come down through the air to see her, and that pleased her very much! So they sat side by side and he told her stories about her eyes. They were (he said) like beautiful dark pools in which thoughts floated like mermaids. And then he told her about her forehead, which was a snow mountain with magnificent halls and paintings. And he also told her about the stork, which brings sweet little babies. What enchanting stories they were! And then he proposed to her and the princess said yes, instantly.

"But you must come here on Saturday," she said. "The king and queen will be taking afternoon tea with me and they will be very proud to hear that I am marrying a Turkish god. But please see that you have a really beautiful story to tell, for my parents are extremely fond of stories. My mother likes moral, refined tales but my father prefers jolly ones that make him laugh."

"Very well," he said, "I shall bring no other wedding present than a story." And so they parted. The princess gave him a sword set with gold coins – and he certainly was going to make good use of those!

The merchant's son flew off and bought himself a new dressing-gown. Then he returned to the woods, sat down, and began to make up a story for the king and queen. It had to be ready by Saturday and that was by no means an easy task. But at last Saturday came and he *was* ready.

The king and queen and the whole court were waiting to take afternoon tea with the princess. The young man was most graciously received.

"Now will you tell us a story," said the queen, "one that is full of meaning and instructive."

"But one which can make me laugh as well," said the king.

"Oh yes," said he, and he told his story. Let us listen very carefully.

"There was once a bundle of matches which were excessively proud because they had come from a most distinguished family. Their family tree was the most lofty tree in the forest and each match was a tiny chip from it. These matches were now lying on a shelf between a tinder-box and an old iron pot and it was to these two that they recounted the story of their young days.

'Ah yes,' they said, 'when we were on the green boughs we really did live well. Every morning and evening we had diamond-tea – dew, you know – and all day long we had sunshine (when, that is, the sun was shining) and all the little birds had to tell us their stories. And you could easily see that we were rich because our family could afford to wear green suits both in summer and winter, while other trees dressed only in summer. But then the woodcutters came – the great revolution, you know – and our family was broken up. The trunk obtained a position as mainmast on a splendid ship which could sail round the entire world if it wished. The other branches of the family went to various places, and we were given the task of lighting fires for ordinary folk. That is the reason distinguished people like us have turned up here in the kitchen.'

'My way of life was different,' said the iron pot, which stood next to the matches on the shelf. 'From the very moment I came into the world I have been scoured and put to boil countless times. I look after people's solid needs and I really am the top person in the house. My one delight, after the table's been cleared, is to sit, clean and trim, on the shelf and to have sensible conversations with my companions. For, apart from the water-bucket, which every so often goes down into the yard, we all live indoors. The only one to bring us any news is the shopping-basket, but it talks somewhat alarmingly about the government and the nation. Only recently an old earthern pot fell down in a fright, shattered to pieces. That shopping-basket is a trouble-maker, I can tell you that!'

'You talk too much,' said the tinder-box, and the steel struck at the flint till the sparks flew out. 'Now how about having a jolly evening?'

'Yes,' said the matches, 'let's discuss who is the most distinguished person here.'

'No, I don't like talking about myself,' said the pot. 'Let's arrange an evening's entertainment. I will begin. I shall talk about something that is familiar to all of us, so that we can all put ourselves into the situation, and that should be very pleasant:

'Near the Baltic Sea, amid the Danish beech groves' (began the pot) . . .

'That's an excellent beginning,' interrupted the plates, 'this is definitely a story we are going to enjoy!'

'Yes, it was there I spent my childhood,' (continued the pot), 'living with a quiet family. The furniture was polished, the floors scrubbed, and clean curtains were put up every fortnight.'

'How interestingly you tell your story,' said the feather-duster. 'One can tell at once that a lady is telling it, there is something so pure and refined running through it.'

'Yes indeed, one does get that feeling,' said the water-bucket, and it gave a little jump of pleasure so that there was a "splash" on the floor.

The pot continued its tale and the end was just as good as the beginning. The plates clattered with delight and the feather-duster got some parsley out of the sand-hole and crowned the pot with it, for it knew this would annoy the others, and 'besides,' it thought, 'if I crown her today, she will crown me tomorrow.'

'And now we are going to dance,' said the tongs, and dance they did! Heaven preserve us! How they kicked their legs up in the air! The old chair-cover in the corner split just watching it!

'May we be crowned?' asked the tongs, and they were.

'Vulgar rabble! that's all they are!' thought the matches.

The tea-urn was now invited to give a song but it had caught a cold, it said, and couldn't sing unless it was brought to the boil. But it was only giving itself airs; the truth was that it would sing only if it were on the table in the presence of its master and mistress.

Over on the window-sill was an old pen, which the maid used to write with. There was nothing special about it except that it had been dipped too deep in the ink-well and was very proud of it.

'If the tea-urn won't sing,' it said, 'then leave it alone. There's a nightingale outside, in a cage; it can sing. Of course, it hasn't been taught, but we won't say anything nasty about that this evening.'

'I find it highly unbecoming,' said the tea-kettle, which was the kitchen singer and also half-sister to the tea-urn, 'that such a foreign bird should be heard. Is that patriotic? I think the shopping-basket should decide.'

'I am *upset*!' said the shopping-basket. 'I am more upset than you can imagine! Is this a fitting way to spend an evening? Would it not be better to put the house in order? Everyone would then be in his right place and I would lead the dance. That should be something!'

'Yes, let's kick up a real din!' they all cried in unison. But just at that moment the door opened. It was the maid. They all remained still and no one made a sound. But there wasn't a single one of them that didn't think what *it* could have done, and how distinguished *it* was. 'Ah, if only *I* had decided,' thought each one, 'it would *really* have been a jolly evening!'

The maid took the matches and struck them to light the fire. Goodness! How they fizzed and blazed! 'Now,' they thought, 'everyone can see that we are of the highest quality! What brilliance we create! What a flash!' And with that they burned themselves out."

"That was a delightful story," said the queen. "I felt I was really in that kitchen with those matches. Yes! Now you shall marry our daughter."

"Yes, certainly," agreed the king. "You shall marry our daughter on Monday." And from then on they treated the young man as one of the family.

The wedding date was fixed and on the night before the marriage the entire city was illuminated. Buns and pretzels were scattered among the crowds. The lads in the streets stood on tiptoe and shouted "Hooray" and whistled through their fingers. It was all magnificent.

"Well, I suppose I'd better be doing something, too,"

thought the merchant's son. So he bought rockets and sparklers and all the fireworks you can think of and put them in his trunk and flew up into the skies.

Fizz-z-z-z! Whirr-r-r-r! Prr-r-r-r! How they sputtered and blazed and popped! All the Turks down below jumped in the air till their slippers flew around their ears. Such a spectacle in the heavens they had never witnessed in their lives. Now indeed they realised it was a god of the Turks who was to marry the princess.

As soon as his trunk came down in the woods the merchant's son thought, "I'll go into the town and find out how things have gone." After all, it was only natural that he should be curious.

Well! The things people said! Every single person he asked had enjoyed the display in his own way; every one of them had found it delightful.

"I saw the god of the Turks himself," said one. "He had eyes like flashing stars and a beard like foaming water."

"He flew in a mantle of fire," said another, "and the loveliest angel-children peeped out from its folds."

He heard these and many other beautiful things about himself, and the next day was to be his wedding-day. He went back to the woods to get inside his trunk ... but where was it? The trunk was burnt. A large spark from the fireworks had set it alight and it had been burnt to ashes. He would never again fly, never again see his bride.

The princess stood the whole day long waiting for him on the roof. She's still waiting. But where is the merchant's son? He's going around the world telling stories. But they are not half as jolly as the one he told about the matches!

The Shirt Collar

THERE was once a fine gentleman whose only belongings were a boot-jack and a comb. But he had the smartest shirt collar in the world and it is the story of this collar that we are now to hear.

About this time the collar was getting old enough to think of finding a wife, and it so happened that in the wash-tub he met up with a garter.

"My word!" said the collar, "I have never met anyone so slender, so graceful, so charming and so delicate. May I know your name?"

"That I shall not tell you," said the garter.

"Where do you come from?" asked the collar. But the garter was bashful and thought this was too delicate a question to answer.

"You are probably a sort of girdle," said the collar, "probably an undergirdle. I see that you are both useful and decorative, little lady."

"You are not to speak to me!" said the garter. "I don't think I

60

have given you any reason for doing so."

"When one is as beautiful as you are," said the collar, "that is reason enough."

"Refrain from coming too near me," said the garter, "you look far too masculine!"

"I am also a fine gentleman," said the collar. "I possess a boot-jack and a comb." Which wasn't really true – they belonged to his master and the collar was only boasting.

"Kindly refrain from coming near me," said the garter again. "I am not accustomed to it."

"Prudish creature!" said the collar. Just then they were taken out of the wash-tub, starched and hung over a chair in the sunshine. Afterwards they were put on the ironing-board and then came the hot iron.

"Mistress!" said the collar, addressing the iron, "little mistress widow, I'm getting all hot! I'm feeling quite changed! What's happening to my folds! You're burning a hole in me! Ah! Will you be my wife?"

"Rag!" said the iron and passed proudly over the collar, for she imagined she was a steam-engine whose place was on the railway lines dragging carriages. "Rag!" she repeated.

The collar was now getting frayed round the edges so the scissors appeared and cut off the loose ends.

"Oh!" said the collar, as soon as he saw the scissors, "you must be a prima ballerina. How well you extend your legs. It's the most charming thing I've seen! There's no one in the whole world to match you!"

"Yes, I know that," said the scissors.

"You deserve to be a countess," said the collar. "And all I possess is a smart gentleman, a boot-jack and a comb. If only I had a title!"

"He can't be proposing to me, surely," said the scissors, and she was so enraged she gave the collar a sharp cut, which made him unfit to be worn.

"I'd better propose to the comb, I suppose," said the collar. "It's extraordinary how you retain all your teeth, little lady. Have you ever considered getting engaged?"

"Yes indeed!" said the comb. "Surely you knew I was engaged to the boot-jack."

"Engaged!" said the collar. Now there seemed no one left to propose to, so he dropped the matter.

A long time passed and the collar finally turned up in a bag at the paper mill, among a large bundle of rags. Those of a better quality kept to themselves, separate from the coarse ones, as is only right and proper. They had a lot to talk about, the collar most of all, for he was a real boaster.

"I've had an awful lot of sweethearts," he said. "I wasn't given a moment's rest. At that time I was a smart gentleman, and starched at that! I had a boot-jack and a comb, which I never used. Oh, you should have seen me when I was laid on my side – I looked really elegant! Never will I forget my first love! She was a girdle, so graceful, so soft and so delicate! For my sake she flung herself into the wash-tub. There was a widow, too, who glowed with passion! But I ignored her and she went black. And then there was a prima ballerina. She was the cause of the scratch which I still bear. She was quite fierce! My own comb was in love with me. She lost all her teeth because she felt crossed in love. Ah yes! I've been through many things like that! But what caused me most upset was the garter – I mean the girdle – throwing herself into the wash-tub. Yes, I have a lot on my conscience. I deserve to be turned into white paper!"

And that, indeed, is what became of him. All the rags were made into white paper, but the collar became the very sheet of paper which you have in front of you now, and on which *this story* is printed. And all because he boasted so much in his later years about things that never really happened. And that should make us think, so that we should never behave like that collar, for we can never know whether *we* shan't end up in the rag bundle and be made into white paper and have our whole history printed on us – yes, even the most personal things! And then have to roam all over the place telling everybody about it, just as the collar did!

The Princess on the Pea

THERE was once a prince who wanted to marry a princess, a *truly real* princess. So off he went travelling all over the world looking for one, but there was always something that wasn't *quite* right. For although there were lots and lots of princesses, the prince could never be absolutely certain whether they were *real* princesses or not; there was always something that didn't quite click. So back he came from his travels, very sad indeed, for he had so wanted to find a *real* princess.

One night there was a terrible storm – thunder and lightning and pouring rain – it was quite frightening. And in the middle of it all there was a violent knocking at the front door and the old king himself went to open it. And there outside stood a princess. But goodness me! What a sight she was, what with all that wind and rain! Water ran down her hair and clothes, trickling in

Now they could see that she was a real princess

through the toes of her shoes and out again at the heels. But she insisted she was a *real* princess!

"We can soon find out about that!" thought the old queen, though she didn't actually say anything to the wet lady outside. She went up to the spare bedroom, removed all the bedclothes from the bed and put one pea on the bedstead. Then she got twenty mattresses, put them on top of the pea and then put a further twenty eiderdowns on top of the mattresses.

And in this bed the princess was to pass the night!

Next morning they asked her how she had slept.

"Oh shockingly!" replied the princess. "I hardly slept a wink the whole night. I can't imagine what there was in the bed but it must have been something very hard because I'm black and blue all over. It was dreadful!"

Now they could see that she *was* a real princess because only a real princess would have felt the pea through twenty mattresses and twenty eiderdowns. No one except a real princess could be as tender-skinned as that.

So the prince married her, for now he knew for certain that she was a true princess. As for the pea, it was placed in a museum, and you can still see it there, unless someone has taken it away.

How about that for a true story!

Big Claus and Little Claus

ONCE upon a time there were two men who lived in the same village and had the same name – both were called Claus. But one of them had four horses and the other only one. So to tell one from the other, they called the one who owned four horses Big Claus and the one who owned only one horse Little Claus. And now let's find out how these two got on together, for it is really quite a story.

The whole working week Little Claus had to lend Big Claus his one horse and do the ploughing for him. In return Big Claus would help Little Claus with his four horses – but only *once* a week, on Sundays. And you should have seen how Little Claus would crack down his whip on those five horses on Sundays, when they were his! The sun shone bright, the church bells pealed out loud and clear and people in their Sunday best, hymn-books under their arms, would walk by on their way to church to hear the vicar preach his sermon. And they would see Little Claus ploughing away with five horses. And he would feel so happy that he would bring down his whip with a resounding "thwack!" and cry: "Gee-up there, all my horses!"

"Don't *say* that," warned Big Claus. "Only one of them is your horse."

But as soon as anyone passed by again on the way to church, Little Claus would forget about this and cry out: "Gee-up there, all my horses."

"Now stop that at once, do you hear," warned Big Claus again. "If you say it just once more I'll crack your horse over the head and kill him dead. And that'll be the end of him."

"I won't say it again, I promise," said Little Claus. But when the people walked by and nodded "Good-day", he felt so happy and so grand to have five horses that he cracked his whip and cried: "Gee-up there, all my horses."

"I'll teach you to gee-up your horses," said Big Claus and, taking a mallet, he brought it down with such a mighty crack on the head of Little Claus's only horse that it fell down dead on the spot.

"Oh, dear," wailed Little Claus. "Now I haven't got a horse at all." And he started to cry. But he didn't cry for long. He stripped the hide off his dead horse and left the hide to dry in the wind. Then he put it into a bag, threw the bag over his shoulder and set off to sell the horse-hide in the nearest town.

He had a long way to go, through a very dark wood, and to make matters worse a sudden most terrible storm blew up. Little Claus lost his way in the darkness and wandered all over the place, till at last he found himself outside a large farmhouse. The shutters were up for it was already nightfall, but he could see a small light shining over the top of them.

"I expect they will put me up for the night," thought Little Claus and he went and knocked at the door.

The farmer's wife opened it, but when she heard what he wanted she said, "You can't come in here. My husband is away and I don't admit strangers." And with that she slammed the door in his face.

Little Claus looked round. There was a haystack close by and between that and the farmhouse there was a shed with a flat thatched roof.

"I can sleep up there," thought Little Claus, looking up at the roof. "It should make a fine bed. I don't imagine that stork will fly at me and peck my legs." (For, standing on the roof, was a real stork which had built its nest there.)

So he climbed on to the shed and lay down and wriggled about till he was nice and comfortable. Then he noticed that the shutters on the farmhouse windows did not quite fit at the top, so he could look over them, right inside, and see what was going on.

What he saw was a big table spread with roast meat and red wine and some tasty looking fish. The farmer's wife and the parish priest were sitting there and she was filling up his glass and he was helping himself to the fish, to which he seemed more than usually partial.

"Wouldn't I just like to have some of that!" thought Little Claus, stretching his head as close to the window as he could. "Goodness me! What a splendid cake! What a feast they're having!"

Just then he heard the sound of horses' hooves along the high road. They were coming towards the house: it was the woman's husband arriving home. He was a most worthy man but he had one rather strange weakness – he couldn't stand the sight of parish priests. The mere mention of one would send him mad with rage, which was why the priest was visiting the farmer's wife when her husband was away, and why she was now offering him her tastiest dishes. So when they heard her husband coming they both got very frightened and the woman told the parish priest to hide in a large empty chest in the corner. This he did at once and the farmer's wife quickly put away all the delicious food and wine in her oven, for if the farmer had seen it he would certainly have asked what it all meant.

"Oh, what a shame," sighed Little Claus from his thatched bed when he saw all the appetising food disappear into the oven.

"Who is that up there?" called the farmer, looking up at Little Claus. "Why are you lying up there? Come indoors with me."

Little Claus then told him about the storm and how he had lost his way, and he asked the farmer if he could put him up for the night.

"Most certainly," said the farmer, "but first let's have supper."

The farmer's wife was now all friendly and welcomed Little Claus when she saw him at the door with her husband. She spread the cloth on the long table and served them a large bowl of porridge. The farmer ate heartily enough but Little Claus could not take his mind off the delicious roast meat and fish and wine and cake which he knew were in the oven. Now, under the table at his feet was the bag with the horse-hide. He trod on the bag and the dry hide gave out a loud squeak.

"Hush!" said Little Claus, pretending to be listening to something, and he trod on it again, making it squeak even louder.

"Hullo," said the farmer, "what's that you've got under there?"

"Oh, that's my wizard. I keep him in my bag," replied Little Claus. "He says we are not to eat the porridge because he's conjured the whole oven full of roast meat, fish, cake and red wine."

"What! What!" exclaimed the farmer, and stretching over to the oven, he opened it and saw all the delicious food his wife had hidden away there but which he believed the wizard had conjured up for him.

His wife, not daring to say a word, placed all the food on the table at once and they helped themselves freely. When they had eaten and drunk to their hearts' content, the farmer became quite jolly and asked: "What else can your wizard do? Can he call up the Devil, I wonder? I'd like to see him do that."

"Oh yes," said Little Claus, "my wizard will do anything I ask – won't you?" and he trod on his bag again. "Did you hear him say yes? But the Devil is not very pretty and I shouldn't bother to see him if I were you."

"Oh I'm not afraid," said the farmer. "What does he really look like?"

"Well, as far as I know, he may well show himself looking like a parish priest."

"Ugh!" grunted the farmer with a start. "I can't stand the sight of parish priests. But no matter, as long as I know it's the Devil I shan't mind. I'm quite brave – but don't let him come too near me."

"I'll ask my wizard then," said Little Claus, and he trod on his bag and bent down to listen.

"What does he say?" asked the farmer.

"He says: 'Go over to the chest in the corner and you'll find the Devil crouching inside.' But hold the lid firm so that he doesn't slip out."

The farmer went over to the chest, lifted the lid and peeped inside.

"Ugh!" he cried and shrank back. "He looks the very image of our parish priest. What a horrid sight!" And then they drank some more wine to get over the shock, and in fact they went on drinking all night.

"You know, you'll have to sell me that wizard of yours," said the farmer. "I'll pay you as much as you like – a whole bushel of money, just say the word."

"Oh no!" said Little Claus. "Just think of all the things he can do for me."

71

"Oh please," begged the farmer, "I simply must have that wizard. I'd give anything in the world for him."

"Oh very well then," said Little Claus. "As you've been kind enough to give me a night's lodging, you can have my wizard for a bushel of money, but I insist on a full measure."

"Of course," said the farmer, "but please see that that chest is taken away. I won't have it in my house a moment longer. He may still be inside," he added with a shudder.

Little Claus gave the farmer his bag with the dry horse-hide and in return received a whole bushel of money, full measure. The farmer also gave him a wheelbarrow to wheel away the money and the chest.

"Goodbye," said Little Claus, and off he went, pushing the barrow with the money and the chest – and the parish priest inside!

He reached the other side of the forest where there was a deep, swift-flowing river. A fine new bridge had been built across it and when he was about halfway across Little Claus said, loud enough for the parish priest to hear, "Now what am I to do with this silly old chest? It's no use to me. I'd better heave it into the river and get rid of it." And he took hold of one end and lifted it up a bit.

"No, stop!" cried the parish priest from inside the chest. "Let me out! Let me out!"

"Ugh!" cried Little Claus, pretending to be scared. "He's still there! I'd better drop it straight into the river and drown him before he gets out."

"Oh no!" pleaded the parish priest. "Let me out and I'll give you a whole bushel of money."

"Well that's different," said Little Claus, opening the chest and letting out the parish priest. Little Claus pushed the chest into the river and the priest ran home and came straight back to give Little Claus another whole bushel of money.

"I seem to have got a good price for that horse of mine," he said to himself when he got home and counted out his gains. "Big Claus will be none too pleased when he finds out how rich I've grown from my one horse."

Soon after this he sent a boy over to Big Claus to borrow a bushel measure. "What on earth can he want that for?" wondered Big Claus, and he stuck a bit of tar at the bottom of the measure so that whatever Little Claus was measuring would stick to it. And indeed that is just what did happen. For when the measure was returned to Big Claus there were three gleaming silver florins sticking to it.

"What *does* this mean?" said Big Claus, and he dashed straight off to Little Claus. "Where have you got all this money from?" he asked.

"Oh, that's from the horse's hide which I sold yesterday."

"And a handsome price you must have got for it," said Big Claus. He hurried back to his house, took an axe and struck all his four horses down dead. He then stripped off their skins and drove to town with them.

"Skins, horse-skins! Who'll buy my horse-skins!" he shouted as he drove through the streets. The tanners and shoemakers came out and asked what price he was asking for them.

"A bushel of money per piece," he replied.

"A bushel of money!" they cried in amazement. "Are you mad?" "Do you think we are fools?" And they took their straps and leather aprons and began to beat him and thrash him until they had chased him right out of town.

"Out of the town with him!" they cried, and Big Claus had to hurry off as fast as he could. Never had he had such a thrashing.

When he got home that night he was very angry. "Little Claus will pay for this," he kept muttering. "He'll pay with his life for this. I'll kill him."

Just about this time Little Claus's old grandmother died. It's true she hadn't been very kind to him (at times she had even been quite nasty), but he felt sorry all the same and so he took the dead lady over to his own warm bed to see if he could bring her back to life again. He left her there all night while he went and slept on a chair in a corner of the room.

In the middle of the night the door opened and in crept Big Claus with his axe. He made straight for the bed and hit the dead grandmother on the head, thinking it was Little Claus.

"Well, that's finished him," he muttered. "He won't make a fool of me again." And he went off home.

"Well, well," said Little Claus. "What a nasty, wicked man! He meant that blow for me. It's a good thing old Grandmother was dead already or he'd have well and truly done the job himself."

He then dressed his grandmother in her Sunday best, borrowed a horse and cart from his neighbour and propped the old lady up on the back seat so that she couldn't slump out if he drove too fast. Then he started out through the forest. He reached an inn just about sunrise and went inside to get a bite of something to eat.

Mine host the innkeeper was a very rich and very pleasant man on the whole, but there were times when he could get very peppery and lose his temper completely.

"Good morning," he said to Little Claus. "I see you're out early today, and in your very best clothes, too."

"Yes," said Little Claus. "I'm off to town with my grandmother. She's sitting out there in the back seat of the cart. She won't come in, so would you kindly take her out a glass of mead. And speak up loud, won't you, as her hearing isn't all that good." The innkeeper poured out a large glass of mead and went out with it.

"Here's a glass of mead from your grandson, madam," he said. But the dead lady never said a word and sat perfectly still.

"Can't you hear?" shouted the innkeeper at the top of his voice. "Here's a glass of mead from your grandson," and he shouted the same thing again and again. But as she didn't budge he flew into a terrible rage and threw the glass right into the dead lady's face. The mead ran down her cheeks and nose and she slumped over the side of the cart – for Little Claus had only propped her up, not tied her fast.

"Now look what you've done!" shouted Little Claus, rushing out of the inn and seizing the innkeeper by the shoulder. "You've gone and killed my poor grandmother! Just look at that great cut in her forehead!"

"Oh, what a terrible thing to happen!" exclaimed the innkeeper, wringing his hands. "And it's all because of my nasty temper. Dear Little Claus, I will give you a whole bushel of money and have the lady buried as though she were my own grandmother. Only don't say anything about it, of course, or they'll cut off my head, and that wouldn't be at all pleasant."

And so Little Claus got yet another bushel of money and the innkeeper buried the old grandmother as if she had been his own.

When Little Claus got back home he sent a boy over to Big Claus to ask if he could borrow a bushel measure.

"My goodness! What can this mean?" wondered Big Claus. "Didn't I kill him? I'd better go and see for myself." And off he went to Little Claus with the bushel measure.

"Where on earth did you get all this money?" he asked, his eyes nearly popping out of his head when he saw what Little Claus had brought home.

"You didn't kill me," said Little Claus. "It was my grandmother you killed with your axe and I've sold her for a bushel of money."

"My goodness, that's a pretty good price you got for her," said Claus and he hurried home and killed his grandmother with his axe. Then he put her in a cart and drove into town to the chemist's and asked him if he wanted to buy a dead body.

"Whose?" asked the chemist, "and where did you get it?"

She slumped over the side of the cart

"It's my grandmother's body," replied Big Claus. "I have killed her and I'm asking a bushel of money for her."

"Heavens above!" exclaimed the chemist. "What next, I wonder! You must be raving mad. If you go about saying things like that, you'll lose your own head. You are a wicked man and you deserve to be punished."

Big Claus was so frightened at this that he rushed out of the shop, jumped into his cart and galloped his horse straight back to his house. The chemist really thought he must have gone mad – and so did everyone else, so they let him drive away and made no effort to stop him.

"You'll pay for this! You'll surely pay for this!" Big Claus kept muttering to himself as he drove along. "You won't escape me this time, Little Claus."

As soon as he was back home he took the biggest sack he could find and went over to Little Claus's house.

"So you've made a fool of me again, have you," he said. "First you made me kill my horses and now my grandmother! You're not going to fool me again!" So saying he seized Little Claus, put him into the sack and slung the sack over his shoulder. "And now, Little Claus," he shouted to him, "I'm going to drown you."

Little Claus was no lightweight and Big Claus had a long way to go before he arrived at the river. Along the road they passed a church where they could hear people singing hymns to the accompaniment of a beautiful organ. "It might be nice if I went in and heard a psalm or two before I go any further," thought Big Claus. So he put down his sack and went into the church.

"Oh dear, oh dear!" sighed Little Claus inside the sack. And he twisted and turned for all he was worth but he couldn't get out.

Just at that moment an old cattle drover came past, driving a herd of cows and bullocks with a big stick which he held in his hand. One or two of them stumbled against the sack and knocked it over.

"Oh dear!" sighed Little Claus, "I'm too young to be going to heaven!"

"And I'm so very old," answered the drover, "and can't get there yet."

"Open the sack!" cried Little Claus. "Change places with me and you'll go to heaven straight away."

"Gladly will I do that," said the drover and he undid the sack and out sprang Little Claus.

"You *will* look after my cattle, won't you," pleaded the drover, creeping into the sack. Little Claus tied up the sack and went off with the cattle.

Soon after, Big Claus came out of the church and flung the sack over his shoulder, thinking how light it had become – the old drover was less than half the weight of Little Claus. "He seems to have grown light as a feather," he muttered to himself. "It must be the effect of that nice hymn I have just sung." Then he made for the river, which was deep and wide, and threw in the sack with the drover inside.

"Take that, Little Claus!" he shouted, "you'll not fool me any more."

Then he set off home, but at the crossroads whom should he meet but Little Claus himself, driving a herd of cows and bullocks.

"What can this mean?" wondered Big Claus. "Didn't I just throw you into the river?" he asked him.

"Yes, you did," answered Little Claus. "You threw me into the river about half an hour ago."

"So where did you get all these fine cattle?" asked Big Claus.

"They're sea-cattle," said Little Claus. "Let me tell you the whole story. I want to thank you very much for drowning me, for now I'm a rich man, believe me. I was terribly frightened when I was in that sack, and how the wind did howl when you

BIG CLAUS AND LITTLE CLAUS

threw me over the bridge into the cold water. I went straight to the bottom, of course, but I didn't get hurt because I fell on to the softest of soft grass that grows on the river bed. The sack was opened by a most beautiful girl in a snow-white dress with a green garland on her wet hair. She took me by the hand and said, 'Is that you, Little Claus? Here are some cattle for you, and a mile further on you will find another herd.' I then saw that the river was a wide sea road for the sea people. They were walking along it down at the bottom, making their way up the bed to the country, where the river ends. I can't tell you how pleasant it was down there, with lovely flowers and fresh green grass and fishes darting past like birds in the air. The people were so friendly and there were so many cattle walking about in the ditches."

"Then whatever made you come up again so soon?" asked Big Claus. "I should have stayed down much longer, as it seems so pleasant down there."

"Well," replied Little Claus, "just listen to me and see how clever I am. You remember I told you that the sea-girl said there was another herd of cattle waiting for me about a mile further on. Well, I know the river bends and winds all over the place so I decided to make a short cut by coming up on land and then diving down into the river again. That way I would save a couple of miles and get the cattle all the quicker."

"You *are* a lucky man, I must say," said Big Claus. "Do you think I could get some sea-cattle if I went down to the bottom of the river?"

"I don't see why you shouldn't," replied Little Claus. "But don't ask me to carry you to the river in a sack, you are far too heavy for me. If you care to walk there and then get into the sack, I'll throw you in with the greatest of pleasure."

"Thank you very much," said Big Claus, "but if I don't get my sea-cattle when I get down there, you can look out! I'll give you the thrashing of your life!"

"Oh please don't be too hard on me," said Little Claus, and

with that they set off to the river. When the cattle saw the water, they ran towards it as fast as ever they could for they were very thirsty.

"You can see how eager they are to get to the bottom again," remarked Little Claus.

"Yes, yes," said Big Claus impatiently, "but hurry up and help me or else you'll get that thrashing I promised you." He then crawled into a big sack which had been lying on the back of one of the herd. "Now put a large stone in it in case I don't sink," he said, as his head disappeared into the sack.

"Yes indeed," said Little Claus, and he put a big stone into the sack, tied the cord fast and gave it a big push. Splash! Down went Big Claus and sank straight to the bottom.

"I'm very much afraid he won't be getting any cattle," said Little Claus and he drove back home with what he had got.

The Wild Swans

IN a distant land, far, far away, where the swallows fly when we are having winter, there lived a king who had eleven sons and one daughter, Elisa. The eleven brothers went to school with stars on their breasts and swords at their sides. They did their writing on golden tablets, with pencils of diamond, and they knew their lessons just as well without their books as with them. You could tell at once that they were princes. Their sister used to sit on a stool made of mirror glass and look at a picture book which cost more than half a kingdom.

The children really did have a wonderful time, but alas! it was not to be like that for long.

The king, their father, had married a second time and the new queen was a wicked queen who was not at all kind to the children – you could tell that from the very first day. There was great feasting and merrymaking on the wedding day and the children played at pretending to be visitors. But the new queen did not give them any of the delicious cakes or sweet apples that they were usually given for their games. No, she gave them sand in a teacup and told them to pretend with that.

The following week the queen sent little Elisa away to the country to stay with some peasants, and before very long she had made the king believe so many false things about the poor princes that his heart was turned against them, too, so that he stopped caring about them.

"Fly out into the world and look after yourselves," the evil queen told them. "Fly out like great big birds which have no voices." But still she could not make her spell as evil as she would have liked it to be: the princes turned into eleven beautiful wild swans and with a curious cry they flew out through the palace windows over the park and into the woods.

It was still quite early in the morning when they flew over the place where their sister Elisa lay sleeping in the peasants' hut. They soared above the roof, flapped their wings and turned their long necks this way and that, but no one heard or saw them, so they flew on and on, higher and higher into the clouds, far into the wide world and thence to a great dark forest that stretched right down to the sea-shore.

Poor little Elisa was in the peasants' hut playing with a green leaf; that was the only toy she had. She made a hole in the leaf and looked at the sun through it and she felt she was looking at the bright eyes of her brothers; and whenever the warm sun shone on her cheeks, she thought of all their kisses.

And so the days went slowly by. The winds blowing through the rose bushes outside the hut whispered to the roses, "Who can be more beautiful than you?" And the roses shook their heads and replied, "Elisa". And when the old peasant woman sat by her doorway on Sunday reading from her hymn-book, the wind would rustle the pages saying, "Who is gentler than you?" And the reply came, "Elisa". And what the roses and the hymn-book said was the pure truth.

When she reached the age of fifteen, Elisa was summoned back home to the palace. The queen saw how beautiful she was and she was filled with rage and hatred. She would certainly have liked to turn Elisa into a wild swan like her brothers but this she did not dare to do because the king wished to see his daughter.

Early in the morning the queen went to her bathroom, which was made of marble and adorned with soft cushions and splendid carpets. She fetched three toads, kissed them and said to one, "Sit on Elisa's head when she gets into the bath so that she may become as slow-witted as you are." And to the second toad she said, "Sit upon her brow so that she may become so ugly that even her father will not recognise her." And to the third toad she said, "Rest upon her heart so that her mind becomes evil and she may suffer pain and torment." And then she put the toads into the clear water (which immediately turned green), summoned Elisa, undressed her and made her get into the bath. As she sat in the bath, the first toad climbed into her hair, the second on to her forehead and the third on to her breast. Elisa did not seem to be aware of them, but when she stood up three red poppies were floating on the water. If the toads had not been poisonous and kissed by the witch, they would have changed into red roses. All the same, they were still flowers, and this was because they had been resting upon Elisa's head and heart. She was too gentle and innocent for witchcraft to have any real power over her.

When the evil queen saw this, she rubbed poor Elisa all over with walnut-juice so that she became a most unpleasant colour, and then she applied a vile ointment to Elisa's beautiful face and disarranged her hair so that it was a tangled mess. No one could possibly have recognised Elisa now. And so when her father saw her, he really had quite a fright and said she wasn't his daughter at all. Nor would anyone have anything to do with her except the watchdog and the swallows, but these poor creatures had nothing to say to her.

The unhappy child wept and thought of her eleven brothers, who were all so far away. With great sadness in her heart she crept out of the palace and for the whole day she wandered over fields and moors and then into the great forest. She had no idea where she wanted to go, but she felt so downcast and longed so much to see her brothers, who, like herself, had been driven out into the wide world, that her only wish was to search until she found them.

She was now far from any road or path, and as it was getting dark she said her prayers and lay down on the soft moss, resting her head against the stump of a tree. The air was mild and still and all around, in the grass and moss, there were hundreds of glow-worms, gleaming like some green fire. And when she happened to touch a bough with her hand they fell like falling stars around where she lay. All that night she dreamed of her brothers. They were children again, playing together, writing on their golden slates with their diamond pencils and reading their wonderful picture book, which had cost half a kingdom. But they weren't writing letters and words as they used to formerly; no, they were writing about their bold exploits and all the exciting things they had seen and done. And in the picture book everything seemed to come alive: the birds sang and the people stepped out of the pages and spoke to Elisa and her brothers.

When she awoke the sun was high in the heavens, though she couldn't see it properly through the dense branches of the tall trees; the sun's rays were dancing upon them like fluttering gold gauze. The air was scented with the smell of fresh green grass and the birds very nearly came and perched on her shoulders. She could hear the sound of water splashing, and through an opening in the bushes Elisa could see it – so beautifully clear that every single leaf was reflected in it.

But when she saw her own face in the water she was very

frightened, it was so dirty and ugly. Then she dipped her hand in the water and rubbed her eyes and forehead and lo! her skin gleamed white again! She took off her clothes and bathed in the cool, clear water, after which there was no more beautiful princess than Elisa in the whole wide world.

When she was dressed once more and her hair all smoothly plaited, she ran to the sparkling spring and drank from the palm of her hand. Then she wandered further into the forest, not quite knowing where she was going.

Everything was so perfectly still she could hear her own footsteps and every withered leaf as it crushed under her feet. There were no birds, at any rate, she couldn't see any. Nor could she feel any sunrays, for the foliage was so rich and dense. She lay down to sleep in the darkness of the forest, thinking all the time of her brothers and wondering if she would ever find them.

The next morning she got up and continued her walk through the forest. She met an old woman carrying a basket of berries. The woman gave her a few and then Elisa asked her whether she had seen eleven princes riding through the forest.

"No, my dear, I have not," replied the old woman, "but yesterday I did see eleven swans with gold crowns on their heads swimming down the river not far from this very spot." And she led Elisa a bit further on towards a slope. At the bottom of this slope was a winding brook. Elisa thanked the old woman and then continued to walk along the brook till it finally opened out on to the wide sea shore. She stared for a long while at the innumerable pebbles on the beach, all washed round and smooth by the water. "The sea never seems to get tired," thought Elisa. "Its waters keep rolling on, making the rough stones smooth, and I, too, will not tire in my search for my dear brothers."

Scattered among the seaweed washed up by the tide she found eleven swans' feathers, which she gathered up into a little bundle. The tiny drops of water on them might have been dew or perhaps tears – she could not tell. Strangely enough, she did not feel lonely as she watched the ever-changing colours of the sea. A great black cloud floated by, and the sea seemed to say, "I, too, can look angry."

Just as the sun was setting Elisa saw eleven wild swans with gold crowns on their heads flying towards the land. Like a long ribbon of white they came in, one behind the other, and Elisa climbed up the slope and hid behind a bush. The swans alighted quite close to her, flapping their great white wings.

As the sun disappeared into the water, the swans' skins peeled off and, lo and behold! there stood Elisa's brothers, eleven handsome princes! She gave a loud happy cry and sprang into their arms and called them by their names. And how happy the princes were to see their little sister once more, although she had now grown taller and more beautiful. They laughed and wept and soon they understood how wickedly their step-mother had treated them.

"We brothers," said the eldest, "fly about like wild swans as long as the sun is in the heavens. But when it sets, we assume our human shape. And so at sunset we must always take care to see that we are standing on our feet, for if we were flying then, up there in the clouds, we would come plunging down into the depths below. We do not live here. On the far side of the water there is a land as fine as this but it is a long, long way away. We have to fly across the wide sea and there is no island where we could spend the night. There is but one solitary rock which juts out above the water but it is not very big, and only by standing side by side can we rest on it. If the sea is rough the water leaps up and sprays right over us. But still we are most thankful that this rock is there – and that is where we spend the night in our human shape. If it were not for this rock, we could never visit our homeland because our journey takes two whole days. Only once a year are we permitted to visit our father's home for a short stay of eleven days. We fly over this great forest and we can see the palace where we were born and where our father lives. And we can also see the bell-tower of the church where our mother is buried. But now we have only two more days left and then we must depart, away over the sea to the other beautiful land which is not our home. But how can we take you with us? We have neither ship nor boat ..."

"And how shall I free you?" asked Elisa. And all night long they went on talking without finding an answer, and they slept only for a very short while.

Elisa was awakened by the sound of swans' wings flapping above her. Her brothers had once again been transformed and she saw them rising higher in ever widening circles and flying farther and farther away. But the youngest one stayed behind. He laid his swan's head on her lap and she caressed his white wings. Towards nightfall the other brothers came back and after sunset they were once again in their human form.

"When we leave you tomorrow, dear Elisa," they said, "we dare not return for a whole year. Have you the courage to come with us? All our wings together are strong enough to fly you over the sea with us."

"Yes," said Elisa, "take me with you."

They spent the whole night weaving a net out of supple willow bark and tough reeds and rushes. Elisa lay down on it and when the sun rose and the brothers changed into wild swans, they seized the net in their beaks and flew high up into the clouds with their dear sister who was sound asleep. The sun's rays fell on her face, so one of the swans flew above her head to shade her with his broad wings.

When Elisa opened her eyes they were a long way from land, and she thought she was still dreaming, because it was such a strange feeling to be carried high up above the sea through the clouds. By her side lay a branch of lovely ripe berries and a handful of appetising roots. These had been gathered by her youngest brother and placed there for her to eat. She sent him a grateful smile for she recognised him as the one who flew above her to shade her with his wings.

They were now flying so high that the first ship they saw below them looked like a white seagull on the water. Behind them Elisa saw a huge cloud, like some gigantic mountain, and upon it were cast giant shadows of herself and of the eleven swans. It was a strange spectacle, the like of which she had never seen before, but as the sun rose higher in the heavens and the cloud was left behind, the phantom shadows disappeared.

All that day they flew on and on, but because they had their sister to carry they could not fly as swiftly as they usually did. As the sun began to sink and evening came near, Elisa was filled with a terrible fear, for she could not see their lonely rock anywhere in sight. To add to her terror, a fearful storm was gathering and she felt guilty because she thought her weight was slowing up the pace of the swans. Panic seized her as she thought of them turning into men and crashing down into the sea far below. She murmured a prayer to soothe her fears but she could still see no sign of the lonely rock. Flashes of lightning followed one another in quick succession and mighty gusts of wind drove menacing black clouds towards them.

Suddenly the swans made a downward plunge . . . and Elisa thought this was the end, but soon they were flying straight on again, with the sun more than half below the water. It was only then that she first caught sight of the lonely rock – it was hardly bigger than a seal's head sticking out above the waves. The sun was sinking fast and was just about to disappear altogether below the water when she felt her foot touching the firm ground and she found herself in the midst of her brothers, all standing close together, arm in arm, on the rock. There was just enough space for the twelve of them. The storm still raged and the sea dashed with terrifying violence against their rock-refuge, but they stood firm and felt no fear.

By dawn the storm had died down and as soon as the sun rose

She found herself in the midst of her brothers

the swans flew off from the rock, carrying Elisa with them. Ahead of them they saw a kind of mountain-land, covered almost entirely in ice, and in the centre a mighty palace, towering high and extending more than a mile in length. But this was not the land they were making for. The swans told Elisa that this was the ever-changing cloud palace of the Fairy Morgana, which no human being was ever allowed to enter. Even as Elisa gazed at it, the mountains and palace crumbled to pieces and in their place rose golden-spired churches. And then again, even as she admired the churches, they changed into a fleet of ships. Then the scene altered once more, and then once more again, until finally and suddenly there loomed up a range of magnificent blue mountains, cedar forests and turreted castles. And before the sun had set, Elisa found herself seated on a rock in front of a great cavern covered with delicate creeper. Her youngest brother led her into the cavern. "Here you shall sleep," he said to her. "Perhaps tonight you may dream of a way of freeing us."

"Heaven grant that I may!" said Elisa. And as she lay down to sleep she sent up a prayer. And the dream she dreamt that night was of the Fairy Morgana and the cloud palace over which she had flown with her brothers. The Fairy came out to meet her, enchantingly beautiful, but somehow looking like the old woman who had offered her berries in the forest and who had told of the swans with the golden crowns.

"You have the power to set your brothers free," she said, "but have you the courage to persevere? Do you see these stinging nettles I hold in my hand? They have been picked from among those that grow out of churchyard graves, and only these will be of use to you. Mark that well! They will burn blisters on your skin, but you must not mind that, however painful it may be. Then you must tread on them with your bare feet to break them up and make them into flax. This you will bind and twist and weave into eleven shirts with long sleeves for your brothers.

When you throw these shirts over the wild swans, the spell will break. But mark this well! From the moment you start your task and until it is complete, *you must not speak*. The very first word you utter will pierce your brothers' hearts like a deadly dagger. Their lives hang on your tongue. Mark that well!"

And then she touched Elisa's hand with the nettle. It was as though a flame burned into her and she awoke with the pain.

It was daylight and close by where she had been sleeping was a nettle like the one she had seen in her dream. She left the cave to begin her heavy task. On the churchyard graves she sought out the nettles with her delicate hands. They burnt like fire and raised great blisters on her hands and arms but she did not mind the pain because she knew she was thus helping to free her beloved brothers. With her bare feet she trod down every nettle and then twisted and bound the green flax.

When the sun set her brothers returned and when they found Elisa so silent they were frightened and didn't know what to think. Was it some new spell cast upon her by their evil step-mother? But when they saw her blistered hands, they realised she must be doing it for their sake. The youngest brother wept bitter tears and where his tears fell she felt no more pain and the blisters disappeared.

All through the night she went on with her task for she could have no rest till she had freed her brothers. And all next day, when the swans were away, she sat in silent solitude. She had now finished one shirt and was at work on the second.

While she was thus occupied she heard the sound of a hunting-horn echoing through the mountains, together with the baying of hounds. Fearful, Elisa took refuge in a cave, gathering her nettles into a bundle and hiding them. A great hound leapt out from among the bushes, followed by another and then another. They bayed and kept running backwards and forwards. Soon a whole band of hunters were outside the cave and one of them, he seemed to be the tallest and most handsome, came forward towards Elisa. Never had he beheld a more beautiful girl.

"How come you to be in this cave, fair maiden?" asked the king (for indeed he was the king). But Elisa simply shook her head and said not a word, for she knew that if she spoke it would cost her brothers their lives.

"Follow me," said the king, "you may not stay here. If you are as good as you are beautiful, I will clothe you in silks and velvets and set a golden crown on your head and you shall come and live in my grandest palace." And the king lifted her up on to his horse. Elisa wept and wrung her hands, and as they rode off through the mountains, followed by the huntsmen, he said to her, "It is only your happiness I want. One day you will thank me."

The sun was now setting and in front of them lay the splendid royal city with its churches and domes. The king led Elisa to the palace but she had no eyes for its magnificence and sumptuous beauty. She wept and felt that nothing would relieve her grief. The women of the palace dressed her in rich regal robes, threaded precious pearls into her long hair and sheathed her hands and arms in long delicately woven gloves but Elisa remained indifferent to their attentions.

Even so, when she was finally arrayed in all her splendid attire, the whole court was speechless before her dazzling beauty and the king chose her to be his bride. But the archbishop shook his head, muttering in the king's ear that the beautiful forest-girl was a sorceress who had bewitched the whole court and cast a spell on the king's heart.

But the king refused to listen to him and commanded that a sumptuous banquet be prepared and joyous music played, though he was sadly disappointed to see that Elisa remained as downcast and sorrowful as ever.

Then the king led her to a small room adorned with the loveliest green hangings; it looked very much like the cave where the king had first seen her. From the ceiling hung the one shirt which she had finished weaving and on the floor was the bundle of flax she had spun from the nettles.

"Dear child," said the king, "in this room you can occupy yourself with the work you were doing before. You can imagine you are back in your old home."

When Elisa saw these familiar things, a smile came to her lips and the colour to her cheeks. She kissed the king's hand and he pressed her to him. He then left and gave the order for the church bells to peal in honour of the forthcoming royal wedding. The beautiful dumb forest-girl was soon to be crowned queen.

However, the archbishop continued to mutter evil things about Elisa into the king's ear and to spread rumours in the court. The king took little notice and the marriage was soon celebrated with all pomp and ceremony. The archbishop himself, according to the custom of the land, had to place the crown on Elisa's head and he pressed it so hard that it hurt. But there was so much sadness in her heart for her brothers that she felt no pain and no sound came from her lips.

The king was exceedingly kind to her and did all he could to help her; and she came to love him more and more every day. She would most dearly have liked to tell him of her sufferings but she dared not utter a word until her task was completed. Each night she would slip from his side and return to the little green room and continue to weave the shirts for her beloved brothers. But when she started on the seventh shirt, she found she had no more flax, left. She knew she must go down to the churchyard to pick the stinging nettles with her own hand, but how was she to get there? By the light of the moon she tiptoed out into the garden, through the long dark paths and out into the churchyard that lay at the back of the garden. On one of the tombstones sat a circle of hideous creatures, half woman, half snake. They took off their ragged clothing as though they were about to bathe, and with their long skinny fingers they prised open the newly-dug graves, drew out the dead bodies and devoured the flesh. They fixed their evil eyes on Elisa as she passed but she said a silent prayer and they could not harm her. She collected the burning nettles and crept back to the palace.

But one person had seen her, and that was the archbishop, who had remained awake while everybody else lay asleep. He was now certain that the new queen was a witch, using some evil sorcery to make the king and all his people do what she wanted them to do.

The archbishop went and told the king what he had seen and how sure he was that the dumb, beautiful forest-girl was in reality a sorceress. The king did not know what to say. He looked round the church and saw the carved wooden images of the saints on the walls. They seemed to be gravely shaking their heads and saying, "No, Elisa is innocent." But the archbishop insisted that what they were really saying was that Elisa was guilty. Tears rolled down the king's cheeks and his heart became heavy with doubt. That night he could not sleep but he pretended to be sleeping and he saw Elisa get up in the middle of the night and go into the small green room. The same thing happened the next night, and the next. Day by day the king's heart grew more sad and Elisa saw this but did not understand why.

By this time she had almost finished ten shirts and then only one more would remain to be done. But she had no more flax left and, worse still, she had no more stinging nettles. So once more she was forced to go down to the churchyard. The archbishop and the king followed her and saw her pass the hideous serpent-witches sitting on one of the tombstones. The king had to turn his face away, for he imagined Elisa to be one of them.

"The people of the land must judge her," said the king the next day. And the people judged Elisa and decided that she must be burned in fire like a witch.

Elisa was taken from the palace and led to a dark, damp

dungeon, where the wind whistled through the barred windows. They allowed her the nettles she had gathered to use as a pillow, and the shirts she had woven as quilts and blankets. Nothing more dear and more precious than these could have been given to her.

Outside the prison street boys sang jeering songs and there was no one to comfort her with a kind word.

But that evening the youngest of the swans suddenly came flapping his wings outside her barred window, and Elisa wept for she knew that this night might be the last she had left to live. But now her task was nearly complete and her brothers were there. The archbishop came and tried to speak to her but she waved him away with looks and gestures, for nothing must be allowed to interrupt her work. Her tears and pain must not have been in vain, and so the archbishop departed, muttering evil words. But Elisa knew she was innocent and continued her work.

It was still one hour before daybreak next morning when her eleven brothers came to the palace gate and demanded to be taken to the presence of the king. They were told that His Majesty was still asleep and must not be disturbed. The brothers begged and pleaded, and even threatened the palace guards. At long last the king came out.

"What is the meaning of all this?" he asked. Just at that moment the sun rose and the brothers were not to be seen, but eleven swans could be observed flying away.

And now all the people came streaming out of their houses to witness the burning of the witch. Elisa was put in an old cart and dressed in a shift of coarse cloth. She was deathly pale and her lovely long hair hung unkempt about her face. Her lips moved in silent prayer while her hands did not cease weaving away at the eleventh shirt. Even on the way to her death she did not interrupt her work. The people screamed and shouted at her.

"See how the witch mutters! Look at her sitting there with

her vile sorcery! Tear it from her! Tear it into a thousand pieces!"

Just as the mob was getting more and more fierce and surging furiously towards the cart, the eleven swans came flapping down towards her. They perched themselves around her on the cart and fluttered their great wings. The mob was frightened and gave way before them, whispering among themselves, "This is a sign from heaven. She must be innocent!" But they dared not say this aloud. And now the hangman seized Elisa by the hand, but she, with rapid movements, threw the eleven shirts one after the other over the swans and lo! in their place stood eleven tall, handsome princes! But the youngest had a swan's wing instead of an arm, because a sleeve was missing from his shirt which she hadn't quite finished.

"Now I can speak!" cried Elisa. "I am innocent!"

The crowds of people went down on their knees as though before a saint, and then Elisa sank, almost lifeless, into her brothers' arms.

"Yes, she is indeed innocent," cried the eldest brother. And then he told them everything that had happened to them and to her.

Then a wonderful thing took place. Out of the pile of wood and sticks, where Elisa was to have been burned, there rose the sweet scent of myriads of roses. Every single stick had taken root and put out branches; the funeral pyre was now a tall hedge of glistening red roses. There was one that grew out taller and more stately than the rest and this one the king plucked and laid it on Elisa's breast. She opened her eyes, which were now filled with peace and happiness.

Then the church bells pealed out as never before and the king, followed by the eleven princes and great crowds of people, led his queen back to the royal palace.

The Ugly Duckling

IT was glorious out in the country. It was summer. The corn was golden yellow, the oats were green, the hay was stacked up in the green meadows and the stork walked around on his long red legs chattering in Egyptian, a language he had learned from his mother. All around the fields and meadows there were woods and in the midst of these woods were deep lakes. Yes indeed, it was glorious out in the country.

Standing there in the sunshine was an old manor, surrounded by a deep moat, and from its walls right down to the water's edge grew great dock leaves, which were so tall that small children could stand upright under the tallest of them; it was as wild here as in the thickest wood. And a duck was sitting there on her nest, hatching out her little ducklings. But she was getting tired; it was taking such a long time and hardly anyone ever came to pay her a visit. The other ducks preferred to swim about in the water rather than sit under a dock leaf chatting to her.

At last the eggs began to crack one after the other – peep! peep! peep! All the egg yolks had come alive and were popping their heads out.

"Quack! Quack!" said the mother duck and they all hurried out as fast as they could, blinking their little eyes all around them under the green leaves. And Mother Duck let them look to their heart's content for green is good for the eyes.

"What a big world it is!" cheeped all the little ones, for they now had much more room than when they were in the eggs.

"Don't go thinking that this is the whole world!" said their mother. "It stretches far beyond the other side of the garden right into the vicarage, though I've never been that far myself ... Well, are you all here?" And she stood up. "No, I haven't got you all yet, the biggest egg is still there. How long is that one going to take, I wonder. I'm just about fed up with waiting!" And she sat down on it again.

"Well, how goes it?" inquired an old duck, who was paying her a call.

"There's this one egg here. It's taking an awfully long time," said the mother duck. "I just can't get it to hatch. But come and have a look at the others. They are the loveliest ducklings you have ever set eyes on. They're the image of their wretched father, who never comes to see me."

"Just let me have a look at the egg that won't hatch," said the old duck. "Yes, I thought so. You may take my word for it, that's a turkey's egg, all right! I was fooled once like that myself! And I had my pack of troubles with the young ones, I can tell you! They're afraid of the water. I just couldn't get them to go in! I quacked and clucked, but a fat lot of good that did! Just let me see that egg again. Yes, to be sure, that's a turkey's egg, all right! I'd just leave it, if I were you, and teach the other ones to swim."

"Ah well, I think I will sit on it a bit longer," said the duck. "I've sat so long, a few days more won't make any difference."

"It's no concern of mine," said the old duck and off she waddled.

At last the great egg did burst. "Peep! Peep!" said the new-born duck tumbling out. My! he certainly was big and ugly! Mother Duck looked at him. "He's quite appallingly large!" said she. "None of the others looked anything like that! Surely, he couldn't be a turkey-chick! Anyway, we'll soon find out! He's going to go into the water even if I have to kick him in myself!"

The next day the weather was perfect and the sun shone down on all the green dock leaves. Mother Duck and all her family came down to the water. Splash! and in she went. "Quack, quack!" she clucked and in went the ducklings one after the other. The water closed over their heads but up they came again straight away and swam delightfully. Their little legs worked busily away; they were all in the water, even the grey ugly one.

"No, he's no turkey," she said. "Look how well he moves his legs, how upright he holds himself! He's my very own child and no mistake, and he's really quite pretty when you take a second look at him. Come along, all of you now, follow me and I'll take you out into the great wide world and introduce you to the other members of the duckyard. But stay close to me all the time or you may get trodden on. And beware of the cat!"

And so out they all went into the duckyard, where there was a terrible row going on between two families quarrelling over an eel's head. But the cat got it in the end.

"Well, that's how things are in the world," said the mother duck, her mouth watering a little, for she would dearly have loved the eel's head for herself. "Now come along, use your legs properly and don't dilly-dally, and when you pass that old duck over there, be sure to bow your heads politely for she is the most distinguished person here. She has Spanish blood in her veins, that's why she's so fat. And can you see? She has a red band of cloth round her leg, which means she's somebody very special, and it's the greatest distinction a duck can enjoy. It signifies that she's somebody we can't do without, somebody who is looked up to by both men and animals. Come on now! Smarten yourselves up a bit! You must *not* turn your toes in. Well-bred ducklings don't do that, they keep their legs well apart, just like father and mother. Now bow your heads politely and say, 'Quack!'"

And this they did. The other ducks looked round and stared at them and said, loud enough for everybody to hear, "Now we've got this lot to put up with! There's far too many of us here as it is! And whew! just look at that one over there! We're certainly not going to stand for him!" And one duck flew right over to him and bit him in the neck.

"Now you just leave him alone, d'you hear!" said the mother duck. "He hasn't done anything to you!"

"Yes, but just look at the size of him!" said the duck who had bitten him. "And he certainly *looks* odd! He had best be kept in his place!"

"That's a pretty lot of ducklings," said the old duck with the red cloth band round her leg. "All of them, that is, except that ugly thing there. He's not a success, is he? It's a pity you can't hatch him out all over again!"

"I'm afraid there's nothing can be done about it, Your Grace," said the mother duck. "He's none too pretty to look at but he's extremely good-natured, and he's as good a swimmer as any of the others – a little better, even, I dare say. Perhaps he'll grow up less ugly in time and not look quite so gawky. He was in the egg too long, that's his trouble, and it has had an effect on his shape." Then she gave him a peck on the neck and smoothed his feathers. "Anyway," she added, "looks don't matter all that much because he's a drake. He'll turn out all right in the end, he's sturdy enough."

"The other ducklings are presentable enough," said the old Duck. "Well, make yourselves at home, and if you happen to find an eel's head, I'd be grateful if you'd bring it along to me."

And so they made themselves at home. But the wretched little duck which was the last to be hatched and which looked so clumsy was bitten and pushed around and made to look silly both by the ducks and the chickens. "He is too big," they all said. And the turkey-cock, who had been born with spurs and therefore considered himself an emperor, puffed himself out like a ship in full sail and came straight at him, gobbling for all he was worth and getting almost purple in the face. The wretched duckling didn't know where he dared stand or walk and felt quite miserable because he looked so ugly and was the laughing stock of the whole yard.

As the days went by things got worse and worse. The poor duckling was chased around by everyone and even his own brothers and sisters turned nasty towards him. "If only the cat could get at you!" they kept saying and his mother said, "I wish you'd get right out of my sight." The ducks bit him, the chickens pecked him and the girl who fed the poultry never missed giving him a kick.

One day he ran off and flew over the fence, but the little birds in the bushes also made off in terror. "It's because I'm so ugly," thought the duckling and he shut his eyes and flew on farther till he came out on to the great moor, where the wild ducks lived. Here he lay the whole night through, tired and sick at heart.

When he woke up next morning, he saw a whole flock of wild ducks come flying towards him.

"What may you be?" they asked, looking the newcomer up and down, and the duckling bowed his head in greeting, turning his head this way and that, as best he could.

"You *are* ugly and no mistake," they said, "but we don't care as long as you don't marry into our family." Oh, the poor little thing! His thoughts were very far from marrying. All he hoped for was to be allowed to lie in the sedge and drink a little marsh water.

He lay in those marshes for two long days and then along came two wild geese (or rather, two wild ganders, for they were both he-geese). It hadn't been all that long since they'd been hatched and that is, perhaps, why they said the first thing that came into their heads.

"Listen, friend," they said, "you are so ugly we've quite taken to you. Why not come along with us and be a bird of passage? Close by in the next moor there are some delightful wild geese, all waiting to marry and all able to cackle beautifully. Come along and try your luck. Ugly as you are, you might make a hit."

Just at that moment there were two loud bangs and the two wild geese fell down dead in the rushes and the water became red with their blood. Then there were two further shots and whole flocks of wild geese rose up from among the reeds. Then there was another loud report. A great hunt was going on, there were huntsmen lying in wait all around the marshes, and some were perched among the branches of the overhanging trees. Blue gunsmoke rose up like clouds into the dark trees and drifted away slowly over the water. Retriever dogs came splashing their way through the swamp, bending the reeds and rushes in all directions. It was all terribly frightening for the poor duckling; he tried to hide his head under his wing but just at that moment a menacingly big dog came nosing right up to him. Its tongue hung out of its mouth, its eyes gleamed most fearfully and it thrust its muzzle right into the duckling's face, showing its sharp, dangerous teeth and then ... splash! off it bounded without doing any harm to the frightened little creature.

"Thank God!" sighed the duckling. "I am so ugly even the dog can't be bothered to bite me."

And so he lay perfectly still as the gunshots whistled through the reeds and the banging and shooting deafened his ears. Not till late in the day did it become quiet again, but the duckling didn't dare move from the spot where he lay. After waiting several hours he raised his head from under his wing, looked about him and hurried off out of the marsh as fast as he could. Over field and meadow he ran on and on, though a fierce storm had begun to rage so that he had great difficulty in making his way.

Towards evening he came to a broken-down little hut. It was in such a tumbledown state that it didn't know which side to fall and so it remained standing. The wind blew so fiercely that the poor duckling had to sit back on his tail to stop himself being blown away; but the storm got worse and worse. Then he noticed that the door had come off one of its hinges and slanted in such a way as to leave a gap through which he could slip inside. And this he did.

It so happened that an old woman lived in this wretched little hut with her cat and her hen. The cat was called Sonnykins and he could arch his back and purr and his fur would even give out sparks if you stroked him the wrong way. The hen was called Chick Shortykins because of her ridiculously short legs, but she was a good layer and the old woman was very attached to her.

In the morning they very soon noticed that there was a strange duckling in the house, and the cat began to purr and the hen to cackle.

"What's all this then?" said the woman looking around, but she couldn't see all that well and so she thought the duckling was some nice fat duck that had lost its way.

"Ah!" she said, "that's a nice little thing we've caught. Now I'll be able to get some duck-eggs, that is, if it's not a drake! We'll soon tell."

And so the duckling was taken on trial for three weeks – but no eggs appeared. The cat was master of the house and the hen the mistress. "*We* – and the rest of the world," they used to say, as if nobody else mattered. The duckling was not too sure about this, but the hen kept him firmly in his place.

"Can you lay eggs?" she asked.

"No."

"Then kindly hold your tongue."

And the cat said, "Can you arch your back, can you purr and can you flash sparks?"

"No."

"Then kindly refrain from expressing opinions when sensible folk are talking."

So the duckling sat in a corner feeling as sad as sad could be. He thought of the fresh air and the sunshine and felt a sudden longing to swim on the water – so strong was the feeling he had to tell the hen about it.

"What on earth has come over you?" asked the hen. "All these odd notions come into your silly head because you just sit and don't do anything! Lay an egg or purr or something and you'll soon feel yourself again, I assure you."

"But it's really so lovely in the water," said the duckling. "It's grand getting the water over your head and plunging right down to the bottom."

"Oh yes, it must be really grand!" said the hen. "You're crazy, that's what you are! Ask the cat, there's nobody cleverer than he is. Just you ask him whether *he* likes swimming on the water and plunging down to the bottom. And don't ask me what *I* think. Better still, ask your mistress, the old woman. She is certainly the cleverest person in the world. Do you think she has any inclination to go swimming in the water and letting it close all over her head?"

"You don't understand what I mean," said the duckling.

"Well, if *we* can't understand you, who on earth would, I'd like to know! I suppose you fancy yourself cleverer than the cat or the old woman, not to mention me! Get rid of those fancy ideas, child! And show some gratitude for all the kindness that's been shown to you! Haven't you been fortunate to find a warm room and company you can learn something from? No, you are

just a chatterbox. It's no fun associating with the likes of you!
Believe me, what I'm telling you is for your own good. I'm
telling you a few unpleasant truths, that's the sign of a genuine
friend. Come on, now! Make an effort, lay some eggs and learn
to purr and give out sparks!"

"I think I'll go out into the wide world," said the duckling.

"Yes, you do that," said the hen.

So the duckling went off and swam in the water and dived
deep down but all creatures kept away from him because he was
so ugly.

By now it was autumn. The leaves in the forest turned yellow
and brown and the wind whirled them round and round in an
untidy dance. Up in the clouds it looked cold and the air was
heavy with hail and snowflakes and on the fence stood the raven
and squawked out of sheer cold; it made you feel chillier than
ever. The poor duckling felt thoroughly miserable.

One evening, against a glorious sunset, a whole flock of
handsome birds arose out of the bushes; never had the duckling
witnessed anything so beautiful. Dazzlingly white they were,
with long graceful necks. They were swans, of course, and, with
a singularly strange cry, they spread their splendid wide wings
and flew off to warmer faraway lands where the lakes do not
freeze. Higher and higher they flew and the ugly little duckling
felt a strange longing as he watched them. He wheeled round
and round in the water, stretched out his neck in the air towards
them and gave out such a peculiar cry that he himself was
frightened by it. Oh, he could never forget those beautiful,
blessèd birds. When they were out of sight he plunged right to
the bottom of the water and when he came up again he felt
stranger than ever. He did not know the name of those birds nor
where they were flying but he loved them more than anything
else he had ever loved before. He wasn't the least bit envious of
them – such loveliness was not meant for him. He would have
been happy if only the ducks had allowed him into their

company – the poor, wretched creature!

And the winter was bitterly cold. The duckling had to swim about in the water to stop it from freezing up entirely. But every night the hole where he swam became smaller and smaller. It froze and the crust of ice crackled, and the duckling had to use his legs constantly to stop the ice from closing in on him. In the end he became quite exhausted and lay quite still, frozen fast in the ice.

Early the next morning a farm worker happened to pass by and spotted him. He went out to him and broke the ice with his wooden shoe and carried the duckling back home to his wife. There he came to life again. His children wanted to play with him but the duckling thought they might do him harm and in his terror flew straight into the milk vat, sending a shower of milk all over the room. The woman screamed and clapped her hands and the duckling flew into a tub where the butter was and from there into a barrel of flour and out again. You can just imagine what a sight he must have looked after all this! The woman was screeching her head off and threw the tongs at him. The children, laughing and yelling, tripped over one another as they tried to catch him. Luckily the door happened to be open and the poor thing was able to fly out into some bushes amid the newly-fallen snow. And there it lay as though in a trance.

It would be too sorrowful a tale to tell you all that the poor duckling had to go through during that harsh winter. He lay out in the swamp among the reeds until at last the sun began to shine again and the larks to sing. It was a magnificent spring.

Once more the duckling stretched his wings, beating the air more vigorously than before, and flew strongly away. And before he could feel the full pleasure of it, he found himself in a large garden full of apple trees in bloom and scented lilac trees whose long green branches hung down over the winding canals. How gloriously beautiful it was here, so full of the freshness of spring! And what is this coming towards him out of the

The woman was screeching her head off

thickets? Three beautiful white swans, their feathers rustling, gliding ever so smoothly over the water! The duckling recognised those splendid creatures and felt overcome by a strange melancholy.

"I will fly over to those royal birds," he thought to himself, "and perhaps they will put me to death for daring to come near them in all my ugliness. But that does not matter. Better to be killed by them than be bitten by ducks, pecked at by hens, chased by the girl who feeds the poultry, or to go hungry through another winter." He flew out into the water and swam towards the beautiful swans. They saw him and came sailing swiftly towards him with rustling wings. "Only kill me," said the poor creature and he bowed his head low against the flat of the water, expecting death. But what was this that he could see in the clear water? He saw beneath him his own image, but no longer that of a clumsy, ugly, grey bird. What he beheld was a snow-white swan! It doesn't really matter if you are born in a duckyard, as long as you've been hatched from a real swan's egg!

And now he somehow felt happy that he had been through all those troubles and hardships for he could feel a greater joy in all the loveliness and good fortune that was ahead of him. The splendid swans swam slowly round him and stroked him with their beaks. Little children came running into the garden and threw bread and corn into the water. The smallest exclaimed, "Look, there's a new one!" And the others shouted delightedly, "Yes, a new one has arrived!" They clapped hands and danced around and ran to their mothers and fathers, and more bread and cake were thrown into the water. "This new one is the most beautiful of them all," they said, "he's so young and handsome!" And the old swans bowed their heads to him.

Then he felt quite shy and covered his head with his wings; he was so happy, he didn't know what to do with himself. But he was not proud, for a kind heart is never proud. And he kept thinking how he had been ill-treated and despised, and now he could hear them all saying that he was the most beautiful of all the birds! The elder tree bent down its branches over the water before him, and the sun shone warm and bright. He rustled his feathers, raised his slender neck and in the joy of his heart he thought, "Little did I dream of such great happiness when I was the Ugly Duckling!"

The Tinder-Box

A soldier came marching down the highway – one, two! One, two! One, two! One, two! He had his knapsack on his back and his sword at his side, for he had been fighting in the wars and now he was on his way back home. By and by he met an old witch. She was fearfully ugly and her lower lip hung right down on her breast.

"Good evening, soldier," she said. "You've a fine sword by your side, I see, and a big knapsack on your back. You look a real soldier! And I'll tell you what, you can have as much money as you want!"

"I thank you for that, old witch," said the soldier.

"D'you see that great tree over there?" asked the witch, pointing to one close by. "It's all hollow inside. Climb up to the top and you'll see the hole. You can slide right down and get to the bottom of the tree. But first I'll tie a rope round your body so that I can hoist you up again when you holler for me."

"What must I do at the bottom of the tree?" asked the soldier.

"Get money!" said the witch. "When you reach the bottom of the tree, you'll see that you're in a long passage. It won't be dark for there are more than a hundred lamps burning down there. You will see three doors. There are keys in the locks, so you'll be able to unlock them. Go into the first room and in the middle of the floor you'll see a big chest with a big dog sitting on it. He's got eyes as big as teacups, but you needn't take any notice of that. I'm giving you my blue-checked apron. Just walk briskly up to the dog, spread my apron out on the floor and sit him on it. Then open the chest and take as much money as you like. It will be all copper. But if you'd sooner have silver, you will have to go into the next room. There you'll see a dog with eyes as big as mill-wheels, but don't take any notice of that. Just sit him on my apron and take as much silver as you like. Now if it's gold you're after, you'll have to go into the third room. There you'll see a dog with a pair of eyes you've never seen so big – each eye is as big as the Round Tower. He's some dog, take my word for it! But you needn't take any notice of that. Just sit him on my apron and he won't do you any harm. And then you can take as much gold as you please."

"That doesn't sound at all bad," said the soldier. "But what do I have to give you, old witch? I don't suppose I'll be getting all that money for nothing!"

"You're wrong, soldier," said the witch. "Not one single farthing will I take from you. All you have to do is to bring me an old tinder-box, which my grandmother forgot when she was last down there."

"Very well," said the soldier. "Let's get that rope round my waist."

"Here you are," said the witch, "and here's my blue-checked apron."

So the soldier climbed up the tree and let himself down

through the hollow trunk, and there he stood, just as the witch had said, in the long passage with the many hundreds of lamps. Then he opened the first door. Ugh! There sat the dog with eyes as big as teacups glaring at him.

"You're a fine chap, aren't you?" said the soldier, and he sat him on the witch's apron and helped himself to as many coppers as he could get in his pocket. Then he shut the chest, put the dog on top and went into the second room. Heavens! There sat the dog with eyes as big as mill-wheels.

"Don't glare at me like that, you'll get eye-strain!" he said. Then he put the dog on the witch's apron, but when he saw the piles of silver coins in the chest, he threw away all the copper money and filled his pockets and his knapsack with silver. And then he went into the third room. What an awful sight greeted him! The dog in this room really did have eyes as big as the Round Tower and they went round and round in his head just like wheels.

"Good evening to you," said the soldier and touched his cap, for a dog like this he had never before seen in all his life. But he didn't look at him for long because he thought he had better get on with his job. And so he put the dog down on the apron and opened the chest. Heavens above! What an enormous pile of gold there was! There was enough there to buy up the whole of Copenhagen, not to mention all the cake-woman's sugar-pigs and all the tin soldiers, whips and rocking-horses in the world! Yes, this was money all right!

So the soldier threw away all the silver shillings with which he had filled his pockets and his knapsack and gathered up the gold instead. All his pockets and his knapsack and his boots and his cap were so full he could hardly walk. He was certainly not short of money now! He sat the dog back on the chest, shut the door and then shouted up through the tree, "Hoist me up now, old witch?"

"Have you got the tinder-box?" asked the witch.

"You're right," exclaimed the soldier, "I've clean forgotten it."

So back he went again to fetch it and then the witch pulled him up, and there he stood again on the highway, his pockets, knapsack, boots and cap all filled with gold.

"What are you going to do with the tinder-box?" asked the soldier.

"That's no concern of yours," she said, "you've got your money, now give me the tinder-box."

"Hoity toity," said the soldier, "tell me honestly what you're going to do with it or I'll draw my sword and cut your head off."

"No!" cried the witch.

So the soldier cut her head off. And there she lay. Then he tied up all his money in her apron, slung the bundle over his shoulder, stuffed the tinder-box into his pocket and set straight off for the town.

It was a splendid town and the soldier put up at the most expensive inn, demanded the best rooms and ordered only the most select dishes on the menu, as befitted a man who had so much money. The boot-boy who had to clean the soldier's boots thought they were unusually old boots for such a rich gentleman (for he hadn't bought any new ones yet). So the next day he got himself a new pair and also some very smart clothes. The soldier had now become a fine gentleman and people were anxious to tell him about all the exciting things that were going on in their city, about the king and about his pretty daughter, the princess.

"How does one get to see her?" asked the soldier.

"Oh, you won't get to see *her*," they said. "She lives in a great copper castle surrounded by lots of walls and towers. Only the king dares go in and out of that castle, for it has been foretold that she will be married to a common soldier and the king won't stand for that."

"I should like to get a look at her, all the same," thought the soldier, but there was no way he could get permission to.

Still he lived merrily enough; he went to the theatre, drove about in the royal gardens and gave a lot of money to the poor, for he knew quite well, from the bad old days, how hard it is when you haven't got a penny to your name. Now he was well off, he had smart clothes and made any number of friends, who all said what a rare good sort he was and a true gentleman. And this pleased him no end. But as he kept spending money every day and never earned any he very soon found himself with no more than a couple of pence in his pocket, and he had to move out of his smart apartments into a tiny garret under the roof. And furthermore he had to brush his own boots and mend them with a darning needle.

None of his friends came to see him any more, for there were too many stairs to climb.

One evening when it was quite dark and he didn't have enough money to buy a candle, he remembered that there was just a tail-end of one in the tinder-box which he had fetched out of the hollow tree where the witch had helped him down. He brought out the tinder-box and the candle-stump but no sooner had he struck it, making the sparks fly out of the flint, than the door burst open and the dog with eyes as big as teacups stood before him and said:

"What does my lord command?"

"What's the meaning of this?" thought the soldier. "This must be a pretty odd sort of tinder-box if I'm going to get anything I want from it! Get me some money!" he said to the dog and whiz! he was gone, and whiz! he was back with a bag full of coppers in his mouth.

The soldier could see now what a marvellous tinder-box it was. If he struck it once, the dog on the chest with the copper money would come; if he struck it twice, the dog on the chest with the silver would come and if he struck it three times then the one on the gold chest would appear. So back he moved to his smart rooms, dressed in elegant clothes and, of course, all his former friends became very fond of him again.

But once as he sat thinking, he said to himself, "It's a very strange business indeed that no one can get to see the princess. Everyone says how beautiful she is but that's not much help if she's got to stay in the copper castle with all those towers for the rest of her life. There must be some way I can get to see her. Now, where's my tinder-box?" And he struck a light and whiz! in came the dog with eyes as big as teacups.

"I know it's midnight," said the soldier, "but I don't care. I *must* see the princess, even if it's only a little glance."

The dog was out through the door in a flash and before the soldier had time to give it a thought he was back again with the princess. There she was indeed, on the dog's back, fast asleep, and she looked so sweet anyone could see she was a real princess. The soldier couldn't help giving her a kiss, true soldier that he was! Then the dog ran back again with the princess. But the next morning, when the king and queen were drinking tea, the princess told them what an odd dream she had had, about a dog and a soldier. She had ridden on the dog, she said, and the soldier had kissed her.

"Well, that's certainly a very pretty dream you've had," remarked the queen, and she told one of the old ladies of the court to keep watch by the princess's bedside the next night to see if it really had been a dream, or what else it might have been.

But oh, how the soldier longed to see the beautiful princess again! So once more the dog came and took her away, making off as fast as his legs could carry him. But the old lady of the court put on her waterproof boots and ran after him just as fast. And when she saw both of them vanish into a big house, she thought, "Now I know where it is," and she drew a great big cross on the door with a bit of chalk. Then she went back home to her bed. But the dog also went back with the princess and when he saw the big chalk cross on the door of the house where the soldier lived, he went and chalked crosses on every single door in the

There she was indeed, on the dog's back, fast asleep

town. This was very cunning because now you couldn't really tell one door from the next.

First thing next morning the king and queen and the old lady of the court, together with other officials, went in procession to find out where the princess had been.

"This is it!" exclaimed the king pointing to the first door with a cross on it.

"No, my dear husband, this is it!" exclaimed the queen, catching sight of another door with a cross on it.

"But there it is over there," and "Here it is over here," they all kept saying, for wherever they looked they could see nothing but doors with crosses on them. So they gave up the search.

But the queen was a very clever woman who could do more than just drive about in a coach. She took her huge gold scissors, cut a large length of silk into pieces and out of these she made a neat little bag. This she filled with fine flour and tied it to the princess's back. And finally she cut a little hole in the bag so that the flour would spill out all along whichever path the princess might follow.

That night the dog turned up once again, took the princess on his back and carried her to the soldier, who loved her more than ever and would dearly have liked to be a prince so that the princess could be his wife.

The dog did not seem to notice that the flour was emptying out all along the way from the castle to the soldier's room, and so he went on running as on the previous night. When morning came, the king and queen could see all too clearly where their daughter had been. The soldier was seized and thrown into jail.

There he sat. Ugh! How dark and gloomy it was! "Tomorrow they will come and hang you," they told him. This was no joke, and what was worse, he had left his tinder-box at the inn. In the morning, through the iron bars of his little prison window, he could see the people hurrying to the place where he was due to be hanged outside the town. He could hear the roll of drums and the steps of the soldiers marching. Everybody seemed to be up and about, and among them the soldier spotted a shoemaker's boy with his leather apron and slippers. He was running so fast that one of his slippers flew off and came bang against the iron bars through which the soldier was gloomily staring.

"Hey there, boy!" he called out. "Why all the hurry? There'll be nothing much to see till *I* get there! But if you run back to the inn where I used to live and fetch me my tinder-box, I'll give you four shillings for your trouble. But you must run as fast as your legs will carry you!" The lad was only too eager to earn a few shillings so he ran and fetched the tinder-box . . . And now, just wait and see what happened.

On the outskirts of the town they had set up a great gallows. Round about stood soldiers and thousands and thousands of people. The judge was also there, and the council and, of course, the king and queen on a splendid throne.

The soldier climbed the ladder, but when he stood on the platform and they were just about to put the rope round his neck, he called out, "I must remind you that, like any other criminal, I am allowed one innocent request before my execution. I should very much like to smoke a pipe of tobacco – it will be my last smoke in this world."

The king couldn't very well say no to this and so the soldier took his tinder-box out of his pocket and struck fire. And then! One two – three – up sprang all three dogs: the one with eyes as big as teacups, the one with eyes like mill-wheels and the one with eyes as large as the Round Tower.

"Save me now," cried the soldier, "otherwise they'll hang me."

The dogs made a dash for the judge and the council, seized one by the leg another by the nose, another by the shoulder, and tossed them so high up in the air that they all fell down and broke to bits and pieces.

"You won't get me!" cried the king, but the biggest dog got hold of him and his queen and tossed them up like the others. The soldiers got scared and everybody started shouting, "Little soldier, you shall be our king and marry the lovely princess!"

They sat the soldier in the king's coach and all three dogs danced in front of it and cried, "Hurrah!" The young lads whistled through their fingers and the soldiers presented arms. The princess came out of her copper castle and was made queen, and you may imagine how pleased she was with that! The wedding feast went on for a whole week; the three dogs sat at the table and made huge eyes at everyone.

Thumbelina

ONCE upon a time there was a woman who dearly wished to have a wee little child but she didn't know where to get one. So she went to an old witch and said to her, "I wish so much to have a little child. Will you not tell me where I may get one?"

"Oh yes," said the witch, "we can do that. Here's a barleycorn for you – not the sort that grows in farmers' fields or that chickens eat. Put it in a flower-pot and you'll soon have something to look at."

"Thank you very much," said the woman, and she gave the witch twelve pence, went home and planted the barleycorn. Very soon a beautiful big flower grew out of it, looking just like a tulip. But the leaves were closed tight, as if it were still in bud.

"That's a lovely flower," said the woman and kissed it on its pretty red and yellow petals. And just as she kissed it, the flower opened with a loud pop! You could see it was a real tulip, but right in the centre, on a green stool, sat a tiny little girl, so pretty and so delicate, and not much taller than half your thumb. So the woman named her Thumbelina. She gave her a dainty, polished walnut shell for her cradle, blue violet leaves for mattresses and a rose leaf for her coverlet. There she slept at night but in the daytime she played on the table, where the woman had put a little plate encircled by a whole wreath of flowers with their stalks in water. A large tulip leaf floated on the water and Thumbelina could sit on it and sail from one side of the plate to the other. And she was given two white horse hairs to use as oars. It all looked charming. Thumbelina could sing, too, as prettily as you could wish.

One night as she lay on her pretty bed, a nasty toad hopped inside through a broken pane in the window. It was big and fat and wet and it came hopping on to the table, where Thumbelina lay sleeping under the red rose leaf.

"She would make a nice wife for my son," thought the toad, and so she took hold of the walnut shell where Thumbelina was sleeping and hopped back through the window down into the garden. Nearby flowed a wide brook with marshy, muddy banks, and this is where the toad lived with her son. Ugh! He was vile and ugly, too, like his mother. All he could say was, "Croak! Croak! Brek-croak!" when he saw the pretty little girl in the walnut shell.

"Don't talk so loud!" said his mother, "or you'll wake her. She could easily run away from us, for she's as light as swansdown. We'll put her on one of the big water-lily leaves in the brook, she's so tiny and light it will seem like an island to her. She won't run away then, and in the meantime we shall get the living-room ready under the mud, where you can live and build a bigger house."

Out on the brook there were many water-lilies with broad leaves, that looked as though they were floating on the water.

The leaf that was furthest away was also the largest. The mother toad swam out to it and placed Thumbelina on it in her walnut shell. The poor little thing woke up very early next morning and when she saw where she was she began to cry bitterly, for all round the big leaf there was water and she couldn't possibly reach the land.

The mother toad sat down on the mud and decorated her room with sedge and reeds, ready for her new daughter-in-law. Then she swam out with her son to the leaf where Thumbelina was. They had come to fetch her little bed, which was to be put in the bridal chamber before she herself came there. The mother toad made a deep curtsey in the water before Thumbelina and said, "This is my son. He is to be your husband and you will live happily together down in the mud." "Croak, croak, brek-croak," was all her son could say.

So they took the pretty little bed and swam off with it while Thumbelina sat alone on the green leaf and cried, for she didn't want to live with the nasty mother or to have her ugly son as a husband. The little fishes swimming below in the water had seen the toad and heard what she had said, so they poked their heads up to see the little girl. When they saw her they thought her so beautiful that it hurt them to think she had to go down to the ugly toad in the mud. That must never happen! So they gathered together down in the water round the green stalk that held the leaf Thumbelina was on, and bit away at it with their tiny teeth till the leaf went floating down the brook, carrying the little girl far, far away, where the toads could not reach her. Away sailed Thumbelina past one town after another. The little birds in the bushes saw her and sang, "What a lovely little girl!"

The leaf floated on, bearing her farther and farther away, and in this way Thumbelina travelled far out into the country. A pretty little white butterfly kept hovering around her head and finally sat down on the leaf next to her, for it had taken a liking to Thumbelina, who herself was highly pleased, for now she was out of the reach of the toads. It was so pleasant where she was sailing; the sun shone on the water, making it look like liquid gold. She removed the ribbon from round her waist and tied one end of it round the butterfly and the other end to the leaf, so that now it went much faster.

Suddenly a large cockchafer came flying by. He saw Thumbelina and in a flash fastened his claws round her slender waist and flew up with her into a tree. The green leaf went on floating down the brook with the butterfly attached to it, for it could not free itself. Heavens! How scared Thumbelina was when the cockchafer flew up into the tree with her! But she was sorry for the beautiful white butterfly which she had tied to the leaf – if it could not break free, it would starve to death. The cockchafer, however, was not concerned about that at all. He sat down with her on the largest leaf and brought her honey to eat and told her she was very pretty, though not in the least like a cockchafer.

Soon after, all the other cockchafers in the tree called to pay her a visit. They looked at Thumbelina and the lady cockchafers drew in their antennae and said, "She's only got two legs, it's pitiful! She's got no antennae! Her waist is so skinny! Ugh! She looks more like a human being. How terribly ugly she is!" Yet Thumbelina was, of course, as pretty as a picture. And though the cockchafer who had carried her off still thought her beautiful, when all the others said she was ugly, he, too, now began to think they were right and would have nothing more to do with her – she could go wherever she pleased! They flew down from the tree with her and sat her on a daisy and there she stayed and cried, because she was so ugly that even the cockchafers wouldn't have her. But, of course, she was the prettiest creature imaginable – graceful, delicate, and as transparent as the most exquisite rose leaf.

All the summer through poor Thumbelina lived alone in the forest. She plaited herself a bed of green stalks and hung it up under a large dark leaf so that no rain might fall on her. She gathered honey from the flowers and every morning drank the dew which lay on the leaves. In this way she spent the summer and autumn, but then winter came – the long, cold winter. The birds which had sung so sweetly for her flew away on their long journeys. The trees and flowers withered, the large dark leaf which she had lived under shrivelled up and became nothing but a yellow, withered stem, and she felt frightfully cold, for her clothes were now all torn and she herself was so tiny and frail. Poor Thumbelina! Was she to freeze to death? It started to snow and every snowflake that fell on her was like a whole shovelful thrown at one of us – for we are tall while she was barely an inch high. She wrapped herself in a withered leaf but that gave her no warmth. She shivered with cold.

Quite close to the wood where she now was lay a large cornfield, but the corn had been cut long ago and only bare dry stubble stood up out of the frozen earth. To her this seemed like a whole forest to wander through and, oh! how she shivered with the cold! At long last she came to the door of a field mouse's home. It was only a hole in the stubble, but in it the field mouse lived snug and cosy – she had a room full of corn, a fine kitchen and a dining room. Poor Thumbelina stood in the doorway like a beggar girl and begged for a little bit of barleycorn, for she hadn't had anything to eat at all for two days.

"You poor little thing," said the field mouse, for she was really very kind hearted, "do come into my warm room and dine with me." And as she decided she liked Thumbelina, she added, "You are most welcome to spend the winter with me, only you must keep my rooms nice and tidy and tell me stories." Thumbelina did everything the kind field mouse required of her and had a most agreeable time.

"We'll be having a visitor very soon," said the field mouse one day. "My neighbour is in the habit of calling on me every week. He is even better off than I am; he has large rooms and goes about in a splendid black velvet coat. If only you would have him for a husband, you would be well looked after. But he cannot see. You must tell him the prettiest stories you know."

But Thumbelina didn't care for this idea; she didn't want the neighbour for a husband, for he was a mole. He came to pay a visit in his black velvet coat. He was very well-to-do and extremely learned. His manor house, the field mouse had said, was more than twenty times bigger than hers. But in spite of his learning, he had no liking for the sun or for pretty flowers. He spoke ill of them, although he had never seen them. Thumbelina had to sing for both the field mouse and the mole and she sang "Fly away, fly away, cockchafer" and "The monk goes walking in the meadow".

The mole immediately fell in love with her and her pretty voice but he said not a word about it, being a very cautious creature. He had lately burrowed a long passage through the earth from his dwelling to theirs and granted Thumbelina and the field mouse permission to take a walk in it whenever they wished. But he begged them not to take fright at the dead bird which lay in the passage; it had been dead only a few days and was still whole and had all its feathers. It had been buried in the spot where he had dug his passage. The mole then took a piece of rotting wood in his mouth (in the dark this shines just like fire) and lighted the way for them through the long dark passage till they came to the spot where the bird lay. Then the mole pushed his broad nose through the earth ceiling, making a hole which let in the light. There, on the earth floor, lay a dead swallow, its pretty wings pressed fast to its sides and its legs tucked under its feathers. The poor bird must have died of cold. The sight made Thumbelina very sad, for she loved all the birds which had sung so prettily to her through the summer. The mole pushed at it with his short leg and said, "It won't chirp any more. It must be wretched to be born a little bird. Heaven be praised that none of my children will come to this. A bird such as this has nothing except its tweet tweet, and so is sure to die of hunger in the winter."

"Yes indeed," said the field mouse. "You speak like a reasonable man. What *has* a bird got, for all its tweet tweet, when winter comes? It must starve and freeze. Why it is considered such a pretty thing, I really don't know."

Thumbelina didn't say anything but when their backs were turned, she bent down, parted the feathers on the bird's head and kissed the closed eyes. "Maybe this was the one that sang so sweetly to me through the summer," she thought. "What happiness you gave me, dear beautiful bird!"

The mole now stopped up the hole which let the daylight through and escorted the ladies home. But that night Thumbelina couldn't sleep a wink. She got out of bed and plaited a beautiful coverlet of hay, carried it down and spread it round the dead bird. Then she placed some soft cotton, which she had found in the field-mouse's room, against the bird's sides so that it could lie warm on the cold earth.

"Goodbye, beautiful bird," she said, "goodbye and thank you for your sweet song in the summer when all the trees were green and the sun shone so warm upon us." She laid her head upon the bird's breast, but in doing so she got quite a shock, for there was something ticking away inside! It was the bird's heart! The swallow was not dead: it had only been numbed by the cold and now that it was warmed up it had revived!

In the autumn all swallows fly off to warm lands but if one of them lags behind, the cold becomes too much for it, so that it falls down quite dead and is covered by the snow.

Thumbelina was shivering all over; she was so frightened for, compared with her, who was barely an inch high, the bird was really huge. But she plucked up courage, arranged the cotton closer round the poor swallow, fetched a curled mint leaf, which she herself used as a coverlet, and placed it over the bird's head. Next night she stole down to it again, and there it was, quite alive, but so weak that it opened its eyes only for a second and looked at Thumbelina standing there with a piece of withered wood in her hand – for she had no other light.

"Thank you, sweet child," said the sick bird. "I am quite warm now. I shall soon get back my strength and fly off again into the warm sunshine."

"Oh!" said Thumbelina, "but it is so very cold outside. It's snowing and freezing. Please stay here in your warm bed and let me look after you." She brought the swallow some water on a leaf, It drank it and told her that it had scratched its wing on a thorn bush and therefore could not fly as strongly as the other birds when they had set off to fly far away to warmer lands. At long last it had fallen to the ground and couldn't remember any more. It didn't know how it had got where it now was.

But there it stayed all the winter and Thumbelina was very kind to it and became very attached to it. Both the mole and the field mouse ignored it completely; they hated the poor, wretched swallow.

When spring came and the sun had warmed the earth, the swallow said goodbye to Thumbelina. She opened up the hole which the mole had made above and the glorious sunlight poured through. The swallow asked her if she wouldn't like to go away with it: she could sit on its back and they would fly far out into the green woods. But Thumbelina said it would upset the old field mouse if she were to leave like that. "No," she said, "I cannot come."

"Goodbye, kind, sweet girl!" said the swallow and flew away into the sunshine. Thumbelina watched it as it flew further and further away into the distance and tears came to her eyes for she dearly loved the poor swallow. "Tweet tweet," sang the bird and flew off into the green woods.

Thumbelina was very sad. She wasn't allowed to go out into the warm sunshine. The corn which had been sown in the field above the field mouse's house had shot up so high it was like a dense forest to our tiny girl who was barely an inch tall.

"You must set about making your trousseau this summer," the field mouse told her, for their neighbour, the dreary old mole in the black velvet coat, had asked for her hand in marriage.

"You must have both linens and woollens, where you can sit and lie when you are married," the field mouse added.

So Thumbelina was obliged to spin on the distaff, and the field mouse engaged four spiders to weave for her day and night.

The mole came to pay a visit every evening and always talked about how, when the summer was over, the sun wouldn't shine half as warmly as now when it was baking the earth hard as stone. Yes, indeed, when summer was over the marriage with Thumbelina would take place. But she wasn't at all happy for there was nothing whatsoever about the dreary old mole that she could possibly like. Every morning when the sun rose and each evening when it set, she would steal out through the doorway, and when the wind blew through the tops of the corn, allowing her to glimpse the blue sky, she thought how beautiful it must be outside. And she longed to see her dear swallow again. But it never came back; it must have flown far, far away into the green woods.

When autumn came Thumbelina's trousseau was all ready.

"In four weeks time the wedding will take place," said the field mouse, but Thumbelina wept and said she didn't want to marry the dreary old mole.

"Stuff and nonsense!" said the field mouse. "Don't be so wayward or I shall bite you with my white teeth! You'll be getting a first-rate husband. Not even the queen has a black velvet coat like his. And he has lots of things in his cellar, and in his kitchen, too! You ought to thank God for such a husband!"

So the marriage was to take place. The mole was not slow in coming to fetch Thumbelina; she was to live with him deep down under the earth, never to come up to the warm sunshine, for he didn't care for the sun. The poor child was upset beyond words; she was now to say goodbye for ever to the beautiful sun – which she had at least been allowed to glimpse through the field mouse's doorway.

"Goodbye, goodbye, bright sun," she said and stretched her arms high up in the air. Then she walked a little outside the field mouse's house, for the corn had now been reaped and there was nothing left but dry stubble.

"Goodbye, goodbye," she said and put her arms round a little red flower that grew there. "Give my greeting to the dear swallow if you chance to see it."

Suddenly she heard a tweet tweet above her head. She looked up and there was the swallow flying by! When it saw Thumbelina it was overjoyed. She told the swallow how loth she was to have the ugly mole for a husband and how she would have to live deep under the earth where the sun never shone. She couldn't help crying at the mere thought of it.

"The cold winter will soon be upon us," said the swallow. "I am flying far away to warmer lands. Will you come with me? You can sit on my back. Only you must tie yourself tight with your waist-ribbon and then we'll fly far, far away – far from the ugly mole and his dark room, far beyond the mountains to the lands where the sun shines more brightly than here, to lands where there are beautiful flowers and where it is always summer. Please fly away with me, dear, sweet little Thumbelina – you who saved my life when I was frozen in the cellar beneath the earth!"

"Yes, I will come with you," said Thumbelina. She sat herself on the bird's back, placed her little feet on its outspread wings, tied her ribbon fast to one of its strongest feathers and the swallow flew off high in the air, over forests and lakes, over high, ever snow-capped mountains. Thumbelina shivered in the freezing air, so she crept under the bird's warm feathers, only keeping out her little head to gaze at the beauty below.

At long last they reached the warm lands. There the sun

Suddenly she heard a tweet tweet above her head

shone bright and the sky seemed twice as lofty, and in the ditches and on the fences grew the most beautiful green and purple grapes. In the woods hung oranges and lemons, there was a scent of curly mint, and among the woods ran the prettiest children chasing brightly coloured butterflies. As the swallow flew further the scene grew more and more beautiful. Under some majestic green trees near a blue lake stood a palace, gleaming white, built in ancient times, surrounded by lofty pillars entwined with vine leaves. In the tops of these pillars were many swallows' nests and one of them was the home of the swallow which was carrying Thumbelina.

"Here is my house," said the swallow. "Choose for yourself one of the splendid flowers growing beneath it and I will set you down on it and you will be as happy as you could wish to be."

"That will be wonderful!" said Thumbelina, clapping her hands.

Down on the ground lay a huge white marble pillar. It had fallen and broken into three fragments among which grew the most dazzlingly white flowers. The swallow flew down with Thumbelina and placed her on one of the broad leaves. Imagine her astonishment when she saw, in the centre of the flower, a little man, as white and transparent as if he were made of glass! On his head was the most charming gold crown and on his shoulders the prettiest bright wings. He was no bigger than Thumbelina. He was the "angel of the flower" – there was one in each blossom, a little man or a little woman – but this one was the king of them all.

"Goodness me! How handsome he is!" whispered Thumbelina to the swallow. But the little king was frightened by the swallow, for next to him it seemed like some giant bird, while he was so tiny and graceful. But when he saw Thumbelina he was very happy, for she was by far the most beautiful creature he had ever seen. He took his gold crown off his head and placed it on hers, asked her what her name was and

if she would be his wife, for then she would be queen of all the flowers. Here indeed was a real husband! Quite different from the toad's son or the mole with the black velvet coat. So she said yes to the handsome prince, and then out of every flower came a lady or lord, a delight to look upon. Each one brought Thumbelina a gift, but best of all was a pair of beautiful wings from a splendid white fly. They were fastened on to Thumbelina's back, so now she, too, could fly from flower to flower. There was much rejoicing; the little swallow sat in its nest and sang its loveliest song, though at heart it was sad for it loved Thumbelina and wished never to be far away from her.

"You shall not be called Thumbelina," said the "angel of the flower" to her. "It's not a pretty name and you are *very* pretty! We shall call you Maia."

"Goodbye, goodbye," said the swallow and flew away once more, away from the warm lands back to Denmark. There it had a little nest above the window of the house where the man who can tell stories lives. And to him it sang tweet tweet, and that is how he learned the whole story.

The Snow Queen

A TALE IN SEVEN PARTS

Part 1

THE MIRROR AND ITS FRAGMENTS

THIS is the story of a very wicked little troll.

One day, when he happened to be in particularly high spirits, he made a mirror which had a most extraordinary power: everything good that was reflected in it vanished into nothing, while everything ugly and useless looked even worse than it really was. The nicest-looking people looked hideously ugly or stood upside down and had no stomachs. You could not recognise their faces for they were so distorted; one single freckle would be shown spread all over the nose and mouth. The wicked little troll thought this was most amusing. When a kindly thought passed through a person's mind, such an ugly grimace would appear on the mirror that the troll had to laugh at the clever thing he had invented. All the people who attended his school for trolls (for he had established such a school) said that a miracle had been performed: now, they said, for the very first time in the world, you could see what people *really* looked like. They ran about everywhere with the troll's mirror and in the end there was not a single person whose face had not been distorted in it. Then they wanted to fly up to heaven to sneer at the angels, and the higher they flew the more nastily did the mirror grin. Then it started to shake because it was laughing so hard and grimacing so much, and finally it fell to earth where it shattered into a billion billion fragments.

Of course, things then became much worse than before because some of the fragments were hardly as big as a grain of sand and whenever they flew into someone's eye they got stuck there and made things seem distorted, so that the person saw only the bad side of things. Some fragments even got into the hearts of a few people and then a terrible thing happened – these hearts turned into a block of ice. Some pieces of the mirror were large enough to be used as window-panes but you thought twice before looking at what your friends might be doing through *these* panes. Other bits were fashioned into spectacles and things went very badly indeed when people used these spectacles in order to see things straight and get a proper perspective of the world. The nasty troll nearly split his sides with laughter at this, he was so tickled. There are still lots of these fragments flying about in the air and we are now going to hear more about them.

Part 2

A LITTLE BOY AND A LITTLE GIRL

IN a certain large town there were so many houses and people that there wasn't enough room for everybody to have their own little garden and so most people had to be satisfied with a few pot plants. In this town there were two poor children who had a small garden not much bigger than a flower-pot. They weren't brother and sister but they loved each other just as much as if they were. Their parents lived next to one another in two small attics, each having a little window facing its neighbour's. The roof of one house joined the next and the rain-gutter ran along the eaves. You had only to straddle across this gutter to get from one window to the other.

Outside the window the parents of each child had a large box where they grew kitchen herbs and also a little rose tree. They grew splendidly. Now the parents had the idea of placing the boxes across the gutter so that they reached from one window to the other and they really looked exactly like two rows of flowers. Pea plants spread down over the boxes and the rose trees sent out their long twigs which twisted about the windows and bent towards each other. They formed a sort of arch of triumph of leaves and flowers. The boxes were high up, of course, and the children knew they were not to climb up on to them, but they were allowed to step out to each other, sit on their little stools below the roses and play for many a long hour.

In winter this pleasure came to an end. The windows became thick with ice and then they would heat copper coins on the stove and press them against the icy window-pane so they would make splendid round peep-holes. Behind each hole there was a smiling round eye, belonging, of course, to the little boy and the little girl, Kay and Gerda. In the summer they could reach one another in one jump but in the winter they had to climb up and down a long staircase, while the snow came pelting down outside.

"Those are the white bees swarming," said the old grandmother. "Do they have a queen bee as well?" asked the little boy for he knew that real bees have one.

"Yes," said the grandmother, "and she flies where they swarm thickest. She is the biggest of them all and she is never still on the ground; she flies up again into the black cloud. Many a winter night she is to be seen flying again through the streets of the town and looking through the windows, and then they freeze in a curious way so that they look like flowers."

"Yes, I've seen that," said both the children, and they knew that it was true.

"Can the Snow Queen come in here?" asked the little girl.

"Yes, let her come in!" said the boy. "I'll put her on the warm stove and then she'll melt."

Grandmother smoothed his hair and told them some more stories.

In the evening when little Kay was at home and half undressed, he climbed on to the stool and peeped out through the little hole. A few snowflakes were falling outside and one of them, the thickest of them all, remained on the edge of one of the flower-boxes. This snowflake grew larger and in the end it took the form of a lady dressed in the finest gauze made of millions of star-like flakes. She was very beautiful and delicate, but she was made of ice – glittering and dazzling – and yet she was alive. Her eyes flashed like two bright stars but there was neither peace nor quiet in them. She nodded towards the window and waved her hand. The little boy was scared and jumped down from the chair. Then he fancied he saw a big bird flying past, outside in front of the window.

Next day there was a clear frost and soon there was a thaw and finally spring came with the sun shining bright and the green buds peeping out. The swallows built their nests, the windows were flung open and the children sat once more in their little garden high up in the rain-gutter.

That summer the roses bloomed more magnificently than ever. The little girl had learnt a hymn and in it there was something about roses. This made her think of her own roses and she sang the hymn to the little boy, who joined in. The little ones held hands, kissed the roses and admired the gorgeous sunshine. How splendid those summer days were! How very beautiful it was outside among the rose bushes, which never seemed to stop blooming.

One day Kay and Gerda were looking at a book with pictures of animals and birds when – just as the clock struck five in the great church tower – Kay suddenly said, "Oh! I've got a pain across my heart!" and then, "Ouch! there's something in my eye!"

The little girl put her arm round his neck. Kay blinked but no, there was nothing to be seen.

"I think it must have gone," he said, but it had not gone. It was one of those bits of glass that had broken away from the mirror – the troll mirror, you remember, that nasty glass which turned everything great and good into something mean and horrid, and in which all nasty things could be seen more plainly and clearly. Poor Kay had also got a splinter right in his heart which was soon to become a lump of ice. It wasn't hurting him at the moment but it was there all the same.

"Why are you crying?" he asked, "You look so ugly. There's nothing wrong with me, I'm not ill. But look," he exclaimed suddenly, "that rose has been worm-eaten, and this one is all bent. They are ugly things, after all. They look like the boxes they've been planted in." And then he gave the box a good kick and plucked off the two roses.

"What are you doing, Kay?" cried the little girl, and when he saw how frightened she was he pulled off another rose and jumped back into his own window, leaving the good little Gerda to herself.

Not long after, when Gerda came out with the picture book, he said it was only fit for babes in arms; and when Grandmother told them stories he kept interrupting and saying, "But ..." And sometimes he would walk behind her wearing a pair of spectacles and imitating her talking. And this made people laugh for it was indeed very much like her. It was not long before he could imitate the way everyone in the street walked and talked. He could mimic everything about them that was nasty or peculiar, and people said, "That lad has certainly got an unusually clever head on his shoulders." But it was really the glass that he had got in his eye and the glass that lay on his heart. And he would even tease little Gerda, who loved him with all her heart. The games he now played were not at all like the ones he had played before; they were so very clever. One winter's day when the snow was falling he brought out a big burning-glass, held up the corner of his blue coat and let the snowflakes fall on it.

"Now look through the glass, Gerda," he said, and every snowflake got bigger and looked like a magnificent flower or a ten-pointed star. It was a delight to look at.

"Do you see how clever it is?" asked Kay. "Much more interesting than real flowers and there is not a single thing wrong with them. They keep their regular shape until they begin to melt."

Shortly after Kay came in wearing big gloves and carrying his sledge on his back. He shouted to Gerda right in her ear, "I've got permission to go to the big square where the others are playing," and he was off.

Over in the square the most daring of the boys would tie their sledges to the back of a farmer's cart and drive off a good way with it. It was great fun. Once as they were playing, a great sledge passed by. It was painted all in white and in it sat someone wrapped in thick white fur and wearing a rough white cap. The sledge drove twice round the square. Kay then tied his little sledge to it and so was carried away with it. The great sledge went faster than ever and the person driving it turned round and gave a friendly nod to Kay as though they were old friends. But each time Kay wanted to cast loose his little sledge, the stranger turned and nodded and so Kay stayed where he was. This went on until they had driven right out through the town gates. By this time the snow was falling so fast that the little boy could barely see his hand in front of him, but still the great sledge went on and on. He tried frantically to loosen the cords so as to get free of the sledge but it was no use – his own little sled was tied fast to the other and on they drove, swift as the wind. He called out as loud as he could but no one heard him – the snow fell thick and fast and the great sledge sped ever onward. Every so often it gave a leap as if it were flying over hedges and ditches. The boy was terribly scared and tried to say his prayers but all he could remember was his multiplication table.

The snowflakes got bigger and bigger till they finally looked like large white fowls, but suddenly they fell to one side and the great sledge came to a halt. The person who was driving it rose from the seat; the fur cap and coat were made entirely of snow. The person was a lady, very tall and slender and dazzlingly white. She was the Snow Queen.

"We have driven a long way," she said, "but why are you trembling? Creep under my bear-skin." And she seated him by her side in the sledge and wrapped the fur round him; he felt as though he was sinking into a snow drift.

"Are you still freezing?" she asked, and she kissed his forehead. What an icy kiss it was! It went right to his heart, though that itself was nearly a lump of ice! He felt as though he was about to die – but only for an instant and then he felt quite well. He no longer was aware of the great cold all around him.

"My sledge! Don't forget my sledge!" That was the first thing he thought of. It was tied to one of the white fowls which flew behind them with the sledge on its back. Then the Snow Queen kissed Kay once more and little Gerda and Grandmother and everybody at home were all forgotten.

"You shall get no more kisses now," she said, "or I might kiss you to death."

Kay looked at her; a more beautiful face he could not imagine. She no longer looked as if she were made of ice, as she did when she sat outside the window and beckoned to him. He thought she was perfection itself and he felt no fear. He told her he could do mental arithmetic, that he knew how many square miles made up the area of his country and how many inhabitants it had. She smiled all the time. And then he thought that he didn't know half enough of what he ought to know, and he looked up into the great expanse of sky and she flew up with him high into the black clouds, while the storm whistled and roared as though it were singing old songs. They flew over woods and lakes, over sea and land. Down below the icy wind stormed, the wolves howled and the snow sparkled. And above them flew

She was the Snow Queen

the black, screaming crows. But highest of all shone the moon, bright and clear. And Kay could watch the long winter night by its light. By day he slept at the feet of the Snow Queen.

Part 3

THE FLOWER GARDEN AND THE WOMAN WHO KNEW MAGIC

BUT what was happening to little Gerda when Kay did not come back? Where on earth could he be? Nobody knew, nobody could tell her. All that the boys could say was that they had seen him tie his sledge to another large one which had driven down the street and out through the town gate. Nobody knew where he had got to. People wept and poor little Gerda cried bitterly. Then there was a rumour that he was dead, drowned in the river that ran past the town. Oh, those winter days were indeed dark and gloomy, but at long last spring came, bringing warmth and sunshine.

"Kay is dead and gone," said little Gerda.

"I don't believe it," said the sunshine.

"He's dead and gone," she said to the swallows.

But they said they didn't believe it and so, in the end, Gerda herself did not believe it.

"I'll put on my new red shoes," she announced one morning. "Kay has never seen them. And then I'll go down to the river and ask about him."

It was very early. Her grandmother was still asleep, so she kissed her, put on her red shoes and went down, through the town gate, towards the river.

"Is it true," she asked, "that you have taken my little playmate? I will give you my new red shoes if you will give him back to me."

And it seemed as though the waves nodded back. So she took her red shoes, the dearest thing she ever possessed, and threw them into the river. But they fell close to the river bank and the little waves carried them straight back to her, to the land. The river, it seemed, refused to take her most precious possession because it hadn't got little Kay. "I haven't thrown the shoes out far enough," she thought. So she got into a boat that lay among the rushes, crept to the further end of the boat and threw the shoes into the water once again. But the little boat was not moored fast and with her throwing movement she made it float away from the shore. She hurried to try to get out but before she could get back the boat was a few yards from the bank and then it began to drift further and further away.

Little Gerda was scared and began to cry but nobody heard her except the sparrows and they couldn't carry her back to the shore. But they did fly along the bank and tried to comfort her by singing a sort of, "Here we are, here we are!" But the boat drifted on even faster downstream and Gerda sat perfectly still in her stockinged feet. Her little red shoes trailed along behind but they couldn't catch up for the boat went along quite swiftly.

Oh, how pretty it was along the river banks! Beautiful flowers, old trees, and sheep and cows grazing on the slopes. But there was not one single human being in sight.

"Maybe the river will carry me to Kay," thought Gerda, and with this she became more cheerful. She stood up and watched the pleasant green banks as she floated by. After a time she went past a great cherry orchard where there was a little house with unusual blue and red windows and a thatched roof and two wooden soldiers who presented arms to all those who sailed by. Gerda thought they were alive and called out to them but of course they didn't answer. Then the river carried her boat quite close to them and she called again, louder this time. Out of the house came an old, old woman supporting herself on a twisted stick and wearing a large sun-hat painted over with the gayest colours.

"You poor little thing," said the old woman, "how on earth did you get out here on this great river and why have you travelled so far into this wide world?" And with that the old woman stepped straight into the water, hooked her twisted stick to the little boat and drew it to the shore. You can imagine how glad little Gerda was to be on dry land again, though she felt the tiniest bit scared of the strange old woman.

"Come and tell me who you are and how you got here," she said. So Gerda told her everything and the old lady kept shaking her head and saying, "Hum, hum," till Gerda had finished. Then Gerda asked her if she had seen little Kay but the old woman said no, he hadn't been that way but not to worry for he would be sure to come. "You must taste my cherries," said the old woman, "and look at my lovely flowers. Each one of them could tell a story better than you could read in any picture book." She took Gerda by the hand and led her into the house and locked the door.

The panes of glass in the very tall windows were red, blue and yellow and the light shone through them in a strange way in various colours. There were lots of delicious cherries on the table and Gerda was allowed to eat as many as she liked. And while she ate them the old woman combed her hair with a comb of gold, making her locks shine bright and yellow round her sweet little face.

"I've always wanted a dear little girl like you," said the old woman. "We'll get on very well together, you'll see." And as she talked and combed, Gerda thought less and less of her foster, brother Kay. For this old woman was a sorceress, though not a terribly wicked one – she only did a little witchcraft now and then and she wanted to keep little Gerda for herself. So now she went into the garden and touched the beautiful rose bushes with her twisted stick, at which they all sank into the black earth so that you couldn't see where they had been. The old woman was afraid that if little Gerda saw the roses she would remember her own roses and that would remind her of Kay and then she might run away.

Now she took Gerda out to see the flower garden. You can't imagine how beautiful and fragrant-smelling it was. Flowers of every season were there in full bloom, gayer and prettier than in any picture book. Gerda jumped for joy and played about in the garden till the sun had gone down behind the tall cherry trees. Then the old woman put her to bed, and what a magnificent bed it was! The pillows were silken red and stuffed full with violets, and Gerda slept soundly and dreamed beautiful dreams, such as a queen might dream on her wedding night.

The next day she was again allowed to play among the flowers and as the days went by Gerda got to know each one. But although there were so many of them she could somehow feel that one was missing. But which one was it? One day as she happened to be gazing at the old woman's sun-hat she noticed that of all the pretty flowers painted on it the prettiest was the rose. The old lady had forgotten to remove it from her hat when she had made all the others vanish from the garden. But that's the

Gerda flung her arms round it and kissed the roses

way things are when you allow your mind to wander!

"My!" exclaimed Gerda, "aren't there any roses here?" And she wandered among the flower beds and searched and searched but she couldn't find a single rose. She sat down and cried and her tears fell on a spot where a rose bush had sunk into the earth. The warm tears moistened the soil and lo! the bush sprouted up all at once, blooming just as it had before it disappeared. Gerda flung her arms round it and kissed the roses and thought of the ones at home, and of little Kay!

"Goodness me," she exclaimed, "what on earth am I doing! I'm supposed to be looking for little Kay! Might you know where he is," she asked the roses. "Is he dead and gone?"

"He is not dead," they replied. "We have been deep in the ground where all the dead people are but Kay is not among them."

"Thank you," said little Gerda and went off to the other flowers and looking into their cups asked, "Do you know where Kay is?" But none of them knew anything about Kay, they were all busy dreaming about their own stories and how delightful it was to be basking in the sunshine.

What did the tiger lily say?

"Do you hear the drum going Boom! Boom!? It is always the same two sounds, Boom! Boom! Listen to the women's mourning song, listen to the call of the priests. The Indian woman stands in her long, red robe on the funeral pile and flames stretch up around her and her dead husband. But the woman is thinking of the living one in the circle, whose eyes burn even more fiercely than the flames and will burn her body to ashes even more quickly than those flames. Can the heart's flame die in the flames of the funeral pile?"

"I don't understand that at all," said little Gerda.

"That's my story," said the tiger lily.

What did the bindweed say?

"Above the narrow path through the fields hangs an ancient

castle fortress. Dense evergreens cover the old red walls, and up there upon the balcony stands a beautiful maid. She leans over the parapet and gazes down upon the road. No rose hangs more fragrant upon its branch and no apple blossom carried by the breeze floats more gracefully along. Her precious silken gown rustles ... 'Is he coming?' "

"Do you mean Kay?" asked little Gerda.

"I'm only telling my own story," replied the bindweed.

What did the snowdrop say?

"Between the trees hangs a swing held by long ropes. Two pretty little girls in frocks white as snow and with long green silk ribbons on their hats are having a swing. Their brother, taller than his sisters, is standing up in the swing, his arms around the ropes and holding a little saucer in one hand and a clay pipe in the other; he is blowing bubbles. The soap bubbles drift upward as the swing goes to and fro. Their lovely colours keep changing and one is still clinging to the pipe bowl and trembling in the breeze. There's a little black dog, too, standing on his hind legs trying to get on to the swing. But it flies past and the little black dog yelps furiously. The bubbles burst and they laugh at him. A swinging board, a floating picture in foam – that is my song."

"It's all very pretty, I suppose," said Gerda, "but you tell it so sadly and there is no mention of little Kay."

What did the hyacinths say?

"There were three beautiful sisters, oh so delicate and graceful they were! The first one wore a dress of red, the second of blue and the third pure white. In the clear moonlight they danced hand in hand by the still water of the lake. They were not elves, you understand, but real people. Then there blew a light breeze, gently fragrant, and the girls vanished into the forest. The fragrant breeze became stronger and three coffins in which the three sisters lay, floated forth from the depths of the forest, over the lake. Glow-worms gleamed around them like lights at night.

Are the dancing sisters asleep or are they dead? The scent of the flowers tells that they are dead. The bells ring for the dead."

"You make me feel terribly sad," said little Gerda, "and your scent is so strong I can't help thinking the girls are really dead. Ah! does that mean little Kay is dead, too?"

"The roses have been down into the earth and they say 'No'."

"Ding, dong!" rang the hyacinth bells. "We are not ringing for little Kay, we don't know him. We are singing our own song, that's the only song we know."

Then Gerda went to the buttercup, gleaming all yellow among the glinting green leaves.

"You are a little shining sun," she said. "Tell me where I can find my dear playmate."

The buttercup gleamed brighter than ever. What song did it sing? Certainly not one about little Kay.

"In a little yard the heavenly sun shone warm on the first day of spring. Its beams swept down the white wall of the neighbour's house. Close by grew the first yellow flowers – shining gold in the warm rays of the sun. The old grandmother was sitting outside; her grand-daughter, a pretty but poor serving girl, was home on a short visit. She kissed her grandmother. There was pure gold in that innocent kiss. And that's my little story," concluded the buttercup.

"My poor, poor, old granny," sighed Gerda. "How you must be missing me and feeling unhappy because I'm not with you! And about little Kay, too! But it will not be long before I shall be home again, and bringing Kay with me ... Well, I see it's no use asking the flowers where he is. They only know their own song and nothing else."

She tucked up her frock so that she could run faster, but the white narcissus hit her leg as she jumped over it and she stopped to ask, "Might you know anything?" And as she stooped down to listen, this is what it said:

"I can see myself, I can see myself!" said the white narcissus.

"How sweet my scent is! Up in the little garret I see a little dancer. First she stands on one foot and then on the other and sometimes on both and she seems to be kicking at the whole world. But is she *really* there or do my eyes deceive me? She is pouring water out of a teapot on to a bit of stuff she's holding; it's her little bodice. Cleanliness is a good thing! The white frock hangs from its peg; it, too, has been washed in the teapot and dried on the roof. She now puts it on and ties her saffron handkerchief round her neck, and this makes the dress look whiter. Up on your legs! Look how she towers on a stalk! I can see myself! I can see myself!"

"I don't much care for all that," said Gerda. "It's of no use to me." Then she ran to the end of the garden. The door was locked but she tugged at the rusty old lock till it broke off. The door flew open and little Gerda ran barefoot into the wide world. Three times she turned round but nobody was running after her. When she could run no longer she sat down on a big stone. She looked round – summer was over, it was late autumn. That was something you couldn't tell in the garden because the sun was always shining on it and flowers of all the seasons were always in full bloom.

"My goodness!" exclaimed little Gerda. "What a lot of time I've spent there; it's autumn already. I dare not stay any longer!" So she got to her feet and went on her way. Her poor feet felt all sore and tired and everything around her looked bleak and sad. The long willow leaves were all yellow and the mist fell from them in drops of water. Leaf after leaf fell off. Only the sloe-thorn still had any fruit – but it was so bitter it made your mouth all tight. Oh, how grey and gloomy everything was in the wide world!

Part 4

THE PRINCE AND THE PRINCESS

GERDA felt she needed to rest again. Just as she sat down, a great crow came hopping over to her, nodding his head and saying, "Kraw! Kraw! Goo'day to ye! Goo'day to ye!" He wanted to be friends with the little girl and asked her where she was going all alone in the wide world. Gerda understood very well what it meant to be "all alone", and she told the crow the whole story of her life and then asked if he had seen Kay.

The crow nodded thoughtfully and said, "Mebbe, mebbe."

"What? What? Do you really think you might have?" cried little Gerda and she kissed the crow so hard she nearly pressed it to death.

"Careful, dear, careful!" said the crow. "I think it may well be little Kay that I saw but if it was, I think he has forgotten you for the princess."

"Does he live with a princess?" asked Gerda.

"Yes," said the crow, "but listen to me. It's difficult for me to speak your language. If you understood crow-language it would be much easier for me."

"No, I haven't learnt it," replied Gerda. "I wish I had asked Granny to teach it to me. She could speak it."

"Never mind," said the crow. "I'll do my best." And he told Gerda everything he knew.

"In the kingdom where we now are there lives a wonderfully clever princess. She has read all the newspapers in the world and forgotten them again – just shows you how clever she is. She was sitting on the throne the other day (which really isn't all that exciting) when she began to hum a song with words which went: 'Why shouldn't I get myself a husband?' And the princess thought, 'Why, there's something to be said for that,' and so she made up her mind to get married. But the man she would marry would be one who would know how to answer when he was spoken to, not just one who merely stood there looking smart – that's terribly dull. So she summoned all her maids of honour and told them of her intentions; they were delighted. 'I like that,' they said, 'it's exactly what I was saying myself only the other day.' You can trust every single word I am telling you," said the crow. "I have a tame sweetheart; she gets about all over the palace and she told me every single thing." This sweetheart was, of course, a crow, too, for a crow always seeks his mate among other crows.

"The newspapers which appeared straight after this had a border of hearts and the Princess's initials on their pages. They announced that every young man who was good-looking was free to come to the palace and talk to the Princess. And the one who seemed most at home there and who spoke best would become her husband. Yes, indeed," (the crow went on) "you can take it from me. True as I sit here. Young men came in by the dozen and there was a great deal of bustle and to-ing and fro-ing but nothing came of it. They could all talk well enough out in the streets but once through the palace gates, facing guards in their silver livery and footmen in gold, they got all confused. And when they stood in front of the throne before the princess herself, all they could do was to repeat the last word she had said, and she certainly wasn't interested in that! It was just as if they had taken something to make them feel sleepy and they didn't really wake up till they were outside again. I saw a whole queue of them from the town gates to the palace gates," (the crow continued) "and, of course, they got hungry and thirsty but they didn't get even as much as a glass of water from the palace. Some of the brighter ones had brought a bit of bread and butter with them but they didn't offer any of it to the others, they only thought of themselves. 'Let them look hungry,' they thought, 'and the princess won't waste any time on them.' "

"But what about little Kay?" asked Gerda. "Wasn't he among the crowd?"

"Just you be patient," said the crow. "I'm just coming to him. On the third day a little chap without horse or carriage came walking gaily towards the palace. His clothes were shabby but he had long flowing hair and his eyes were as bright as yours."

"That was Kay!" cried Gerda joyfully. "So at last I have found him!" And she clapped her hands.

"He had a little knapsack on his back," said the crow.

"Ah, that would be his sledge," said Gerda. "He went off with it."

"Quite possibly, quite possibly," said the crow, "I didn't examine it very closely. But I do know from my tame sweetheart that when he walked through the palace gates and saw the guards' silver livery and the footmen in their gold he wasn't in the least put out. He just nodded and said, 'It must be dull being on duty at the gates and standing on the stairs all the time. I'd better go in.' The halls glittered with bright lights. Important ministers of state and private secretaries were walking about barefoot carrying golden dishes. You felt there was some solemn ceremony going on. His boots creaked badly but he wasn't in the least bit embarrassed."

"That certainly sounds like Kay!" cried Gerda. "He'd got some new boots, I heard them creak in Granny's room."

"Yes, they most certainly did creak," continued the crow. "But nothing daunted he marched boldly in to the princess herself who was seated on a pearl as big as a spinning-wheel. All the maids of honour and their attendants, and the attendants' attendants, and all the courtiers with their aides, and the aides of these aides, each one of whom was attended by a page, were all standing around. And the nearer they stood to the door the grander they looked. The pages of the aides' aides, who always walk about in slippers, stood so proud you could hardly look at them!"

"It sounds quite terrifying," said little Gerda. "And yet, for all that, Kay won the hand of the princess!"

"If I hadn't been a crow, I'd have married her myself, even though I am engaged. I heard from my tame sweetheart that he spoke as well as I do myself (though I talk in crow-language, of course). He was very good-looking and jolly. It seemed he hadn't come courting at all, but just to hear the princess's wise talk. And he thought very highly of it. And she liked him as well."

"I'm more certain than ever that it's Kay," said Gerda. "He was very clever. He could do mental arithmetic and fractions. Oh, please take me to the palace, too."

"That's easier said than done," replied the crow. "The problem is *how*? I'll have to talk it over with my tame sweetheart, she'll no doubt give me some good advice. I can assure you that a little girl like you would never be permitted to go in."

"Oh yes, I will," cried Gerda confidently. "When Kay knows I'm here he'll come out and take me in."

"Well, just wait for me over there at the stile," said the crow. And with a wag of the head he flew off.

Gerda waited till late in the evening and it was getting quite dark before the crow came back. It greeted Gerda with a "Kraw! Kraw!" and said, "My tame sweetheart sends you this little loaf which she got from the kitchen. I'm sure you must be very hungry. She says you just cannot get into the palace barefoot. The guards in their silver livery and the footmen in gold would simply not allow it. But don't be upset. You'll get in all the same. My tame sweetheart knows a little secret staircase leading up to the bedroom and she also knows where the key is!"

They went into the garden, through the wide avenue where the leaves were falling one after the other. When the palace lights went out, the crow led Gerda to a back door which stood wide open.

Gerda's heart was beating fast with hope and fear. She felt she was doing something she oughtn't to be doing, yet she only wanted to know if it was indeed little Kay inside the palace. Yes, it must be! She could picture his bright eyes and his long hair. She could see him smiling just as he used to smile at home when they sat among the roses. He would certainly be overjoyed to see her and to hear how far she had come for his sake and to learn how much they had all missed him at home. How happy and anxious she felt!

And now they were going up the stairs. There was a little lamp burning on a shelf and right in the middle of the floor stood the tame crow twitching her head from right to left and looking at Gerda who bobbed a little curtsey as her grandmother had taught her to do.

"My betrothed has spoken most favourably of you, dear lady," said the tame crow. "Your life story, if I may call it so, is most touching. If you will kindly take the lamp I will lead the way. We will not be meeting anyone so we can walk straight ahead."

"I feel someone is following us," said Gerda, as something rushed past her, "like shadows on the walls – horses with their manes flying and ladies and gentlemen out hunting on horseback."

"They are only dreams," said the crow. "They come to fetch the Royal visitors' thoughts to the hunt. And that's a good thing for you can look at them more closely in bed. But I hope, when honour and distinction are bestowed upon you, that you will show your gratitude."

"Oh, there's no question about that," said the crow from the forest.

They now came into the first hall, all covered with rose-red satin walls embroidered with artificial flowers. The dreams came darting past even more quickly, so quickly indeed that Gerda could not manage to see the noble lords and ladies. Each room was more sumptuous than the last, it was quite bewildering. And now they were in the bedroom. The ceiling here was like a huge palm tree with leaves of glass, and in the middle of the room there were two beds hanging from a thick stem of gold. Each bed resembled a lily. One of them was white and that was where the princess was lying; the other was red and that was where Gerda was to look for little Kay. She bent back one of the red leaves and saw a brown neck. Oh, it was Kay! She called out his name and held the lamp over him. Once again the dreams came galloping into the room – he awoke, turned his head, and . . . it wasn't Kay!

It was only the neck that looked like Kay's. But the prince was young and handsome and the princess, in her lily bed, opened her eyes and asked what was the matter. Little Gerda burst into tears and told her whole story and all that the two crows had done for her.

"You poor little thing!" said the prince and princess. They praised the crows and said they were not in the least angry with them but they mustn't do it again. And they would get their reward.

"You may either go free," said the princess, "or have a perm-anent post as official crows of the Court. This, of course, carries

She called out his name and held the lamp over him

the right to have everything that is left over in the kitchen."

Both crows made a deep bow and said they would be honoured to accept permanent posts. "We must think of our old age," they said. "It is always wise to have something put by for a rainy day."

The prince then got out of his bed and let Gerda sleep in it. She folded her hands and thought, "How kind men and animals are!" And then she closed her eyes and went peacefully to sleep. All the dreams came flying back again, but this time they looked like angels pulling a little sledge, with Kay sitting in it, and he seemed to be nodding to her. But it was all only a dream.

The next day they dressed her out in silk and velvet and they invited her to stay at the palace and enjoy herself. But all she asked for was a little carriage and horse and a pair of boots. She wanted to drive out into the world and look for little Kay.

They gave her boots and a warm muff, and a carriage of pure gold stood at the door ready to take her off. The coat of arms of the prince and princess gleamed like a star on its doors and the coachmen wore gold crowns. The prince and the princess helped her into the carriage and wished her good luck. The forest crow, who was now married, saw her off for the first few miles. He sat by Gerda's side for he did not like riding backwards, while the tame crow perched herself in the doorway and flapped her wings, but she didn't go with them for she had suffered from headaches ever since she had obtained her permanent post, and she probably ate too many of the leftovers in the kitchen.

"Goodbye, goodbye!" cried the prince and princess. Little Gerda wept and so did the crow, and it went on like this for the first three miles. Then the crow said "Goodbye!" and this was the most painful parting of all. Then he flew up into a tree and beat his black wings for as long as he could see the carriage glittering in the bright sunshine.

Part 5

THE LITTLE ROBBER GIRL

On they drove through the dark forest and the carriage gleamed so brilliantly that it dazzled the eyes of the robbers.

"It's gold! It's gold!" they shouted. They dashed forth, seized the horses, killed the coachmen and postillions and dragged little Gerda out of the coach.

"She is very pretty and well fed by the look of it," said the old robber woman, who had a coarse beard and extremely shaggy eyebrows. "She's as good as a lamb that's been fattened. She'll make a tasty morsel!" And she drew her gleaming knife which shone frighteningly.

"Ouch!" shrieked the old hag all of a sudden, for just at that second she had received a savage bite in the ear from her own rough little daughter who was clinging to her mother's back. "You horrid little brat!" shouted the mother – but it stopped her from killing Gerda.

"I want her to play with me," said the little robber girl. "She'll give me her muff and her pretty frock and sleep in my

160

bed with me." And then she gave her mother another fierce bite which made the woman jump in the air and twirl right round. The other robbers laughed. "Look how she's dancing with her young cub!" they shouted.

"Now I'm going to get into the carriage," said the little robber girl. You could tell she was used to having everything her own way, she was so spoiled and obstinate. And so she sat next to Gerda in the coach as they drove deeper and deeper into the dark forest.

The little robber girl was as tall as Gerda but stronger and broader in the shoulders. Her eyes were jet-black and rather sad. She put her arm round Gerda's waist and said, "They won't kill you as long as I'm not angry with you. They say you're a princess."

"No," said Gerda, "I'm not a princess," and she related everything that had happened to her and how she loved little Kay. The robber girl listened attentively and said, "I won't let them kill you even if I do get angry with you; I'll do it myself!" Then she dried Gerda's eyes and put her hands into the soft, warm muff.

The carriage came to a halt and they were in the courtyard of a robber's castle. There was a big split in the walls from top to bottom. Ravens and crows flew out of the holes in the wall and huge bulldogs, each one big enough to devour a man, jumped up into the air. But they did not bark for barking was forbidden. In the smoky old hall there was a bright fire burning in the middle of the stone floor. An enormous cauldron of soup was boiling away and hares and rabbits were roasting on the spit.

"Tonight you are going to sleep with me and all my pet animals," said the little robber girl. Then they had something to eat and drink and went into a corner spread over with straw and blankets. About a hundred pigeons, apparently asleep, were sitting on perches above them. "They all belong to me," said the little robber girl and she grabbed the nearest one, held it by its legs and shook it till its wings flapped. "Give it a kiss," she cried, beating Gerda's face with it. "Those two over there are rascals," she continued, "they fly off if you don't keep them safely locked up." Then she pulled out a reindeer by its horn. It was tethered to the wall and had a copper ring round its neck. "This is my sweetheart, Baa," she said. "He has to be kept tied up too, or he'd soon be off. Every night I have to tickle him on his neck with this sharp knife and that's enough to keep him scared." And she drew out a long knife from a cleft in the wall and passed it over the animal's neck. The poor creature kicked his legs but the robber girl only laughed and pulled Gerda into bed with her.

"Will you have the knife with you while you're asleep?" asked Gerda, looking at it apprehensively.

"I always sleep with my knife," replied the girl, "you never know what can happen. But now tell me again what you told me before about little Kay and why you've come out into the wide world." So Gerda told her story all over again from the beginning. The robber girl put her arms round Gerda's neck, but she still held the knife in one hand. She slept – you could hear her sleeping – but little Gerda didn't close an eye; she didn't know whether she was going to live or die.

The other robbers sat round the fire, singing and drinking, while the old woman turned somersaults. It was a horrible sight for poor little Gerda.

Then she heard the pigeons saying, "Coo! Coo! We have seen little Kay. A white hen was carrying his sledge and he was sitting in the Snow Queen's carriage which came low over the forest as we lay in our nest. She blew on us young pigeons and they all died except us two. Coo! Coo!"

"What's that you are saying?" asked Gerda. "Where was the Snow Queen flying to. Can you tell me anything about that?"

"I daresay she was going to Lapland," said one. "They always have snow and ice up there. You just ask the reindeer who's tied up over there."

"Yes," said the reindeer, "there is snow and ice in those parts and it's really glorious. You can run about where you like over the great shining valleys. The Snow Queen has her summer tent there, but her castle is up near the North Pole on Spitzbergen Island."

"Oh, poor Kay, poor dear little Kay!" cried Gerda.

"Lie still, will you!" cried the robber girl, "or you'll get a knife in your tummy!"

In the morning Gerda told her all that the pigeons had said. The robber girl looked grave and said, "Well, it's all the same, it's all the same." Then she turned to the reindeer. "Do you know where Lapland is?" she asked.

"Who would know better than I," he said, his eyes all a-sparkle. "I was born and bred there and used to run over the snowfields."

"Listen to me," said the robber girl to Gerda. "All the men have gone out but my mother's still here and she'll be here for some little while, but round about midday she has a drink out of that big bottle and then takes a little nap. When she's asleep I'll do something for you." She jumped out of bed, put her arms round her mother's neck and tugged her beard, crying, "'Morning, old nanny-goat." Her mother smacked her across the nose good and hard till it was red and blue, but it was all done out of affection.

When the old woman had drunk from the bottle and fallen asleep, the robber girl went over to the reindeer and said, "I should like to tickle you a lot more with my knife for that makes me laugh, but never mind. I'm going to untie your tether and let you run free so that you can go to Lapland. But you must make the best use of your legs and carry this girl to the Snow Queen's palace, for that's where her friend is. You heard well enough what she told me for you were eavesdropping."

The reindeer gave a joyful jump. The robber girl lifted Gerda on to his back, gave her a little cushion to sit on and took care to tie her fast. "It's just as well," she said. "Here are your fur boots, it's getting quite cold. But I'm keeping your muff, it's much too pretty. I'm not going to have you freeze, though. Here are my mother's long gauntlets, they'll reach up to your elbow."

Gerda simply cried for joy. "I can't stand your whining," said the robber girl. "You ought to look really happy and in case you get hungry here are a couple of loaves and some ham." She tied these on to the reindeer's back. Then she opened the door, got all the dogs to come inside and cut the tether with her knife. Then she said to the reindeer, "Now run along and see you take good care of this girl."

Gerda stretched out her hand towards the little robber girl and said, "Goodbye," and the reindeer leapt away over bushes and stumps and bog and moor through the dark forest, as fast as he could. The wolves howled and the ravens cawed. "Whish! Whish!" went the reindeer as he leapt up in the air, like a sort of sneeze of red lightning.

"Those are my old Northern Lights," said the reindeer, "just look how bright they are!" And he leapt on faster than ever, day and night, night and day. The loaves were eaten and so was the ham and at last they were in Lapland.

Part 6

THE LAPP WOMAN
AND THE FINN WOMAN

THEY stopped at a small house – a miserable looking little hut it was really. The roof came right down to the ground and the door was so low that the family had to crawl on their stomachs to get in. There was no one in except for an old Lapp woman who was baking fish over an oil lamp. The reindeer told her all about Gerda but first he told his own story because he thought that much more important. Gerda was so exhausted by the cold, she could scarcely speak.

"Ah, you poor creatures," said the Lapp woman. "You've still got a very long way to go. It's more than a hundred miles to Finmark, for that is where the Snow Queen is staying, in the country, and she burns blue lights every single evening. I'll write a few words on a dry cod, for I have no paper, and you can take it to the Finn woman up there. You'll get better instructions from her than I can give you."

So when Gerda had got herself warmed up and had

something to eat and drink, the Lapp woman wrote a message on a dried cod, telling Gerda to take good care of it; she tied her fast to the reindeer again and off he went. Whish! Whish! the noise went high up in the sky, and all through the night the most beautiful blue Northern Lights sent out their blazing gleams.

And so they got to Finmark and knocked at the Finn woman's chimney, for she didn't have a door. But inside there was such a great heat that the Finn woman herself wore hardly any clothes. She was small and not too clean. She immediately loosened Gerda's dress and took off her gauntlets and boots for otherwise she would have been far too hot. She placed a piece of ice on the reindeer's head and read what was written on the dried cod. Again and again she read it through and when she knew it by heart she threw the fish into the saucepan for it would make a good meal and she never wasted anything.

The reindeer then told his own story and when he had finished he told Gerda's. The Finn woman blinked her eyes shrewdly but didn't say a word.

"I know you are very clever," said the reindeer. "You can tie all the winds of the world in one bit of sewing cotton; when the skipper loosens one knot he gets a good wind, if he loosens the second the wind blows hard but when he loosens the third and fourth there's such a storm that the forests are blown down. Will you give the little girl a drink so that she can have the strength of twelve men and vanquish the Snow Queen?"

"The strength of twelve!" said the Finn woman. "That'll go a long way, to be sure!" She went over to a shelf, brought out a great rolled-up skin and unrolled it. It had curious letters written on it and the Finn woman read it till the water ran down her forehead. The reindeer again begged hard for little Gerda and Gerda looked at the Finn woman with such tearful eyes that her own eyes started blinking again. She drew the reindeer into a corner, placed fresh pieces of ice on his head and whispered something to him. This is what she said:

She drew the reindeer into a corner

"Little Kay is certainly at the Snow Queen's and is pleased with everything he finds there. But why is this? Because he's got a splinter of glass in his eye and another tiny piece in his heart. These must be got out somehow or other, else he will never be a human being again and the Snow Queen will always have him in her power."

"But can't you give Gerda something so that she will have power over all this?"

"No, I can't give her any greater power than she's got within her. And her power is pretty great already, don't you see? Men and beasts have to be at her service and she is making her way in the wide world on her bare feet. She must not learn her power from us. Her power is in her heart and in her child's innocence. If she herself cannot get through to the Snow Queen, if she cannot herself get the glass out of little Kay's eye and heart, then we can't be of any help to her. Now listen, two miles from here the Snow Queen's garden begins. Take her there and set her down near the bush which stands out from the snow with its red berries. But don't spend time gossiping there, but hurry up and get back here." And saying that the Finn woman lifted little Gerda on to the reindeer's back and away he went as fast as his legs could carry him.

"Oh, I haven't got my boots nor my gauntlets!" cried little Gerda. She soon noticed it in the biting cold, but the reindeer didn't dare stop. He ran on till he arrived at the bush with the red berries and there he set Gerda down and gave her a kiss. Great clear tears came down the beast's cheeks and poor Gerda stood there without shoes or gauntlets in the terrible, icy cold of Finmark.

When the reindeer left her she ran forward as fast as she could and a vast regiment of snowflakes suddenly appeared. But they seemed not to come from the sky for that was shining clear with the Northern Lights. They came along the ground and the closer they came the bigger they grew. Nearer and nearer they came . . .

they were frightening ... they were alive! They were the Snow Queen's advance guards and were of the strangest shapes and sizes. Some were like ugly porcupines, others like knots of snakes with their heads sticking out, others like fat little bears, their fur all bristling. But they were all white, living snowflakes.

Then little Gerda began to say her prayers and the cold was so intense she could see her own breath coming from her mouth, like smoke. Her breath became thicker and thicker and turned into the shapes of little angels who grew bigger and bigger when they touched the ground. They wore helmets and carried shields and spears. By the time Gerda had finished her prayers a whole army of them stood around her. They attacked the monstrous snowflakes with their spears, shattering them into a thousand pieces, so that Gerda was able to move forward without fear. The angels rubbed her hands and feet so that she felt less cold. She advanced more quickly towards the Snow Queen's palace.

But now let us see how little Kay was getting on. He was certainly not thinking about Gerda nor did he dream that she was standing in front of the palace.

Part 7

WHAT HAPPENED IN THE
SNOW QUEEN'S PALACE AND WHAT
TOOK PLACE AFTERWARDS

THE palace walls had been formed by snowdrifts and the
windows and doors by the cutting winds. There were hundreds
of halls all blown together by the drifting snow. How vast they
were! There was never any fun or jollity in these halls, not even a
ball for the little bears, when the storm might have played the
music while the bears walked on their hind legs and did pretty
tricks. There were never any fun and games, never any little coffee
gathering for the white young lady foxes. All was cold and bare
in the palace of the Snow Queen. The Northern Lights blazed
strong and bright, and with such punctuality that you could tell
when they had reached their highest point, or their lowest. In the
middle of all this there was a frozen lake. It had shattered into a
thousand fragments, but each bit was so exactly like the next that

it was quite an artistic feat. And there in the middle of the lake the Snow Queen would sit when she was at home. And she said that she sat in the Mirror of Reason, which was the *only* one and the best in the world.

Little Kay was blue with cold but he didn't seem to mind, for the Snow Queen had kissed the shivers out of him and his heart was like a lump of ice. He was dragging a few pieces of sharp, flat ice and trying to arrange them into various patterns, just as we try to lay pieces of wood side by side to form a definite shape, a sort of jigsaw puzzle you might call it. He was making the most complicated arrangements – an Ice Intelligence Puzzle. In Kay's eyes these patterns were particularly remarkable, and this was because the fragment of glass stuck in his eye made him see them like that. He was arranging the patterns to try to form a word but he never seemed to manage to get the word quite as he wanted it to be. The word was *Eternity*. The Snow Queen had told him, "If you can discover that pattern you can be your own master and I shall give you the whole world and a new pair of skates." But he couldn't.

"And now I'm off to the hot countries," announced the Snow Queen. "I'm going to have a peep into those black pots" (she meant those two great volcanoes, Etna and Vesuvius) "and I'm going to make them look a bit whiter. This is an important job and it will do the grapes and lemons a lot of good."

So the Snow Queen flew away and Kay was left all alone in the vast ice-cold hall, staring at the bits of ice and thinking and thinking till cracks could be heard inside him. Quite still and stiff he sat, you'd have thought he had frozen to death.

It was then that little Gerda walked through the great gate into the palace. She said a prayer and the biting winds grew calm as though they had fallen asleep. She entered the vast, ice-cold hall and saw Kay. She flew to him, clasped him tight and cried, "Kay! Dear, darling Kay! I have found you at last!" But little Kay sat all stiff and cold and still. Then Gerda's hot tears fell upon his breast and worked their way right through to his heart and melted the lump of ice that was there and ate up the fragment of glass. Then Kay burst into tears and his tears cleared the piece of glass from his eye so that he recognised little Gerda and cried out with great joy, "Gerda, dear, dear little Gerda, where have you been all this long time? And where on earth have I been?" Then looking around he shuddered. "How cold it is here! Isn't it huge and empty!" And he clasped Gerda tight and they both laughed and cried for joy. Even the pieces of ice seemed happy and began to dance. Then after a while they had a rest and then arranged themselves into the pattern which the Snow Queen had asked Kay to make and which would make him his own master.

Then Gerda kissed his cheeks and they bloomed, and she kissed his eyes and they shone like hers, and she kissed his hands and feet and he became strong and well. If the Snow Queen were to return now it would not matter, for the letters were all there in gleaming ice, and Kay was free.

Then they clasped hands and set forth from the great palace of ice. They talked about their grandmother and about the roses on the roof and wherever they went the wind grew calm and the sun broke through. And when they got to the bush with the red berries the reindeer was there waiting for them and he had another young reindeer there whose udders were full and which gave them warm milk. Then they carried Kay and Gerda to the Finn woman where they warmed themselves in the hot room and were told how to get back home. And then the two reindeer took them to the Lapp woman who had made them new clothes and put their sledge right.

The two reindeer leapt along beside them as far as the edge of the country. There they could see the first green shoots sprouting forth and there they said goodbye to the reindeer and thanked them for all their great kindness.

And now they could hear the twittering of the birds and saw

the woods bright with green buds. And out of the woods, on a beautiful horse (Gerda recognised it at once for it was the one that had drawn her golden coach), a young girl came riding. She wore a brilliant red cap and carried pistols at her side. This was the robber girl, who had got tired of staying at home and was setting out towards the north or – if she didn't like it there – in some other direction. She and Gerda recognised each other at once and they were delighted.

"You're a fine one to be chasing about after, I must say," said the robber girl to Kay. "I wonder whether it's worth the trouble running to the ends of the earth to find you!"

But Gerda stroked her cheeks and asked about the prince and princess.

"They've gone travelling to foreign parts," replied the robber girl.

"And what about the crow?" asked Gerda.

"The crow is dead," she replied, "and the tame crow is now a widow and she goes about with a patch of black woollen yarn round her leg. She's a real misery, I can tell you! But it's all show! But now it's your turn to tell me how you got on and how you caught him in the end."

So Kay and Gerda told her the whole story.

"Well, snip-snap-snurr-bass-lurr ..." said the robber girl and she shook their hands and promised that if she ever was passing through their town she'd pay them a call. And then she rode off into the wide world.

Kay and Gerda went on hand in hand, and as they went everything became beautiful with the blossoms and flowers of spring. The church bells rang out and they recognised the lofty towers and the big town. This was where they lived. They walked up to their grandmother's door, went in, climbed the stairs and entered the room where everything was just as it was before. "Tic-toc, tic-toc," the clock was saying and the hands were turning. But as they went from room to room they could somehow feel that they had become grown up. The roses on the roof-gutter were blooming near the open window and there, too, were the children's chairs. They sat down and held each other by the hand. The vast ice-cold splendour of the Snow Queen's palace was now no more than a horrible dream. Grandmother was sitting there as well, reading aloud from the Bible in the bright sunshine.

Kay and Gerda sat there and looked into each other's eyes. They were grown up and yet they were children – children at heart – and it was summer, warm, blessed summer.

The Darning Needle

Once upon a time there was a darning needle who was so fine that she imagined herself to be a sewing needle.

"Just watch what you're holding!" said the darning needle to the fingers that had picked her up. "Don't lose me! Were I to fall on the floor I should never be found again! I am so fine!"

"Quite, quite," said the fingers, gripping her round the middle.

"Just look, I'm coming along with my train," said the darning needle, drawing a long thread (which had no knot) after her. The fingers directed the needle straight towards the cook's slipper, where the upper leather was torn and now had to be sewn together again.

"This is base work," said the darning needle. "I shall never get through! I'm breaking! I'm breaking!" And she did break.

"Didn't I say so?" she said. "I'm so fine!"

"And now she's not fit for anything," thought the fingers.

Still they had to hold her tight all the same, as the cook dropped a blob of sealing-wax on to her, then pinned her to the front of her scarf.

"Look! Now I'm a brooch!" said the darning needle. "I knew I would come to a place of honour! When one *is* something, one always comes to something." And she laughed – to herself, of course, for one can never see from the outside when a darning needle is laughing. So there she sat, as proud as if she were driving in her coach, and looking around on all sides.

"May I have the honour of enquiring whether you are made of gold?" she asked a pin next to her. "You have a handsome exterior and a head of your own, though it's on the small side. You should see that it grows for it is not everyone that has sealing-wax on their ends." And with that the darning needle drew herself up so proudly that she fell out of the scarf into the sink just as the cook was emptying it out.

"Now we are off on our travels," said the darning needle. "I hope I don't get lost!" But she did.

"I'm too fine for this world," she said as she lay in the gutter. "But I am well aware who I am and that always affords one pleasure." And the darning needle held herself straight and kept up her good spirits. All sorts and kinds of things came sailing over her, bits of stick, wisps of straw and old scraps of newspaper.

"Just look at them all sailing along," said the darning needle. "Little do they know what is sticking up just underneath them! It is I! It is I who is stuck firmly here! Look, there goes a bit of wood, thinking of nothing but itself – a bit of wood! And over there, there's some straw. Just watch it twist and twirl. Don't think so much of yourself! You might go bang into a paving stone! There goes a newspaper. Everything on it has long been forgotten and yet it's spreading itself out all the same! I shall sit here patiently and calmly. I know what I am and I shall stay that way!"

One day something gleamed so brightly close by that the darning needle thought it must be a diamond. But it was only a bit of broken bottle. As it shone so brilliantly the darning needle spoke to it, introducing herself as a brooch.

"I take it you are diamond," she said.

"Yes, something like that," was the reply. So each one believed that the other was something really costly, and they talked about the world and how haughty it was.

"Yes, I have lived in a box belonging to a young lady," said the darning needle, "and the young lady was a cook. She had five fingers on each hand but anything as stuck-up as those five fingers I have never known! And yet they were only there to hold me, to take me out of the box and put me back into the box!"

"Did they have any special lustre?" asked the bit of bottle.

"Lustre!" said the darning needle. "No indeed! It was sheer haughtiness! They were five brothers, all of the finger family. They held themselves close together, side by side, though they were of different lengths. The outside one, the thumbling, was short and fat and stood apart from the rest. He had only one joint in his back and could consequently make only one bow. But he claimed that if he was chopped off a man's hand, that man became completely unfit for service. The second finger, lick-pot, was dipped into sweet and sour dishes to determine the taste, and would point to the sun and moon; it was the one that gripped the pen when it wrote. Long-man looked over the heads of the others, while gold-rim wore a ring round its stomach. Little Peter Playman had nothing at all to do and seemed proud of it. They all did nothing but boast and brag ... And then I fell into the wash-tub."

"And here we sit and gleam," said the bit of glass, but just at that moment more water came pouring into the gutter, carrying away with it the bit of broken bottle.

"Well, it seems to have been given promotion," said the darning needle. "But I remain here. I am too fine. But still, I have my pride and it should be respected." So there she stayed, stiff and upright, thinking many thoughts.

"I could well believe that I was born of a sunbeam, so very fine am I! It would seem, too, that the sun was always seeking me out under the water. Ah! I am so fine, even my mother cannot find me! If I had my old eye, which broke off, I think I'd really cry! No! I wouldn't. Crying isn't refined."

One day some lads in the street were rummaging about in the gutter; they found old nails, coins and other such things. It was an awful mess but they liked it.

"Ouch!" said one, who had pricked himself on the darning needle. "Here's a fine fellow for you!"

"I am no fellow," said the darning needle, "I am a young lady." But no one heard her. She had lost her sealing-wax and had turned black, but blackness makes one look slender, so she thought herself even finer than before.

"Here comes an eggshell," said the lads, and they stuck the darning needle into the shell.

"I am black against a white background," said the darning needle. "How matching! People can see me now! If only I don't get seasick! If I do, I shall break!"

But she wasn't seasick and she didn't break.

"It's a good thing with seasickness to have a steel stomach and always to bear in mind that one is rather superior," said the darning needle. "The sick feeling has gone now. The finer one is, the more one can bear."

"Crack!" went the eggshell, for a carrier van had ridden over it.

"Ouch! What a crush!" said the darning needle. "Now I *shall* be seasick! I'm breaking! I'm breaking!"

But she didn't break, although the carrier van had ridden over her.

She lay there, full length, and there let her lie.

The Nightingale

IN China, as you probably know, the Emperor is Chinese and all the people around him are Chinese too. The story I am about to tell you happened many, many years ago but that is precisely why it is worth hearing now – before it gets forgotten!

The Emperor's palace was the most magnificent palace in the world. It was made entirely of fine porcelain, very costly, but so fragile that one had to be careful how one touched it. The most wonderful flowers grew in the garden and on the really gorgeous ones hung little silver bells which tinkled when you passed, so that you were bound to notice them. Everything was artistically arranged in the Emperor's garden, and it extended so far that even the gardener himself did not know where exactly it ended.

But if you kept walking you came to a splendid forest with lofty trees and deep lakes. The forest extended right down to the sea and great ships could sail in beneath the very branches of the trees. And among these branches lived a nightingale, which sang so sweetly that even the poor fisherman, who had so many other things to do, would stop and listen to her song when he came out at night to cast his nets. "How beautiful!" he would think, but then he had to attend to his work and forgot about the bird. But the next night, when the nightingale sang again, the fisherman would again stop still and listen and exclaim, "Oh, what a very pretty song!"

From all the countries of the world travellers came to the Emperor's city and they would admire it and its palace and the garden. But when they heard the nightingale they would exclaim, "There is nothing to compare with this!"

When they went home they would continue to talk about the wonderful bird. Learned men wrote many books about the city, the palace and the garden but they never forgot to mention the nightingale, which they praised most of all. And the poets among them composed the most beautiful verses about the nightingale in the wood by the deep lake.

These books went all over the world and a few of them even reached the Emperor. He was sitting in his golden chair; he read and read and kept nodding his head every minute for it gave him great pleasure to read the flattering descriptions of his city, his palace and his garden. And then he read, "Yet best of all is the nightingale."

"What's this!" exclaimed the Emperor. "I don't know anything about this nightingale! Is there such a bird in my empire, not to mention in my own garden? And I have never heard of it! To think that such things need to be discovered by reading about them in books!"

And so he summoned the Court Cavalier, a person of such exalted rank that when anyone ventured to ask him a question the only answer he gave was, "P!" and that meant precisely nothing at all.

"It appears there is a highly remarkable bird here, called a nightingale," said the Emperor. "They say it is the finest thing in all my empire. Why has nobody ever told me about it?"

"I have never before heard the bird mentioned," said the Court Cavalier. "She has never been presented at court."

"It is my wish that she should come and sing before me tonight," said the Emperor. "Strange that the whole world should know what I possess and yet I know nothing whatever about it."

"Nobody has ever spoken to me of this bird before," repeated the Court Cavalier. "I shall seek her out and find her."

But where was she to be found? The Court Cavalier ran up and down all the stairs, through all the halls, corridors and passages, but not a single person he spoke to had ever heard of the nightingale. So he hurried back to the Emperor and told him it could only be some story invented by the people who write books.

"Your Imperial Majesty would never credit what these people write! It is sheer invention! And there is something else too, something they call the Black Art."

"But the book in which I read this," said the Emperor, "was sent to me by the mighty Emperor of Japan and so it cannot be untrue. I *will* hear this nightingale! She *must* be here this evening! She has my imperial favour! And if she does not come, the entire court's stomachs will be trampled upon just after they've finished supper!"

"Tsing-pe!" said the Court Cavalier and once more he started running up all the stairs and through all the corridors and passages, and half the court ran with him for they did not like the thought of their stomachs being trampled on. Widespread inquiries were made about the remarkable nightingale, which the whole world – except the court – knew about.

At last they came upon a little girl working in the kitchen and she said, "Heavens above! The nightingale? Indeed, I know her very well. How beautifully she sings! Every evening I am allowed to take scraps from the table home to my poor sick mother, who lives down by the shore, and on my way back I sometimes stop and have a rest in the woods and I hear the nightingale sing. And tears come to my eyes and I feel as if my mother was kissing me."

"Little kitchen maid," said the Court Cavalier, "I will get you a regular job in the kitchen and permission to see the Emperor dine if you will take us to where the nightingale is, for she has been summoned to be present before the Emperor this very evening."

So they all went into the wood where the nightingale used to sing. Half the court came along. As they walked along a cow began to moo.

"Oh!" cried the royal pages, "that must be it! What a remarkably strong voice for so small a creature. But surely we've heard it before!"

"Oh no!" exclaimed the kitchen maid, "that's only a cow mooing. We're a long way off yet."

Soon they heard frogs croaking in the marshes.

"Delightful!" said the Chief Court Preacher. "Now I can hear her. It's just like the sound of church bells!"

"No, those are frogs," said the kitchen maid. "But we shall be seeing the nightingale before very long now."

And then the nightingale began to sing.

"That's her!" exclaimed the little kitchen maid. "Just listen! Look! There she is! Sitting up there!" And she pointed to a little grey bird in the branches.

"Is it really possible?" asked the Court Cavalier. "I should never have thought she would look like that. How very ordinary! Perhaps the bird has lost her colour at seeing so many distinguished personages around."

"Little nightingale," called the little kitchen maid, "our gracious Emperor desires that you should sing before him."

"With the greatest pleasure," replied the nightingale, and she

She pointed to a little grey bird in the branches

sang a song that was a delight to hear.

"It sounds just like little glass bells," said the Court Cavalier. "And just look at her little throat working away! Is it not odd that we have never heard her before? She will certainly be a great success at court!"

"Shall I sing again for the Emperor?" asked the nightingale (because she thought the Emperor was there too).

"Most excellent little nightingale," said the Court Cavalier, "it gives me the greatest pleasure to convey to you His Imperial Majesty's invitation to the Court Festival this evening, when you will enchant the Emperor with your lovely song."

"My songs sound best out here in the woods," said the nightingale. Still, as it was the Emperor's wish, she was happy to go along with them.

The palace was right royally bedecked for the occasion. The walls and floors, which were of porcelain, shone in the light of thousands of golden lamps. The loveliest flowers (not forgetting the silver bells tied around them) were arranged along the corridors, so that as people kept rushing hither and thither they created a great draught of air which made the bells ring all the louder and you couldn't hear the sound of your own voice.

A golden perch had been set up in the great hall where the Emperor sat enthroned. It was on this perch that the nightingale was to sit. The entire court was there and the little kitchen maid (who had now received the title of Cook to the Imperial Kitchen) was allowed to stand by the door, where she had a good view of everything that went on. Everybody was grandly dressed and all eyes were turned to the little grey bird. The Emperor gave a nod in her direction as a sign that she should begin.

The nightingale sang so gloriously that tears came to the Emperor's eyes and ran down his cheeks. Then the nightingale sang again, even more sweetly, so that the Emperor's heart melted with joy and sadness. The nightingale, he announced, should wear his own golden slipper round her neck, but the nightingale thanked him, saying that she had already received a sufficient reward.

"I have seen tears in the Emperor's eyes and the tears of an Emperor have a special value. Heaven knows I have been sufficiently rewarded." And then she sang once again, more gloriously than ever.

"It's the most charming love-talk imaginable," said the ladies of the court, and they put water into their mouths so they could gurgle like the nightingale. Even the chambermaids and the valets declared how extremely pleased they were with the nightingale's singing, and this was most important for they are usually an extremely difficult lot to please. In short, the nightingale was a great success.

It was decided that from now on the nightingale was to remain at court and have her own cage and be free to fly out twice every day and once at night. She had twelve attendants, each of whom had a silk string fastened to the bird's leg. This they held on to very tight. There was no joy for the little nightingale in these outings.

The whole city was now talking of the remarkable bird. When any two people met, one of them had only to say "nightin..." and the other would finish "gale". And then they would sigh deeply and with great understanding. No fewer than eleven grocers' children were named after her, though none of them could sing a note.

One day a large parcel arrived for the Emperor, with the word "Nightingale" written on it.

"This must be a new book about our famous bird," said the Emperor. But it wasn't a book. It was a little mechanical thing, in a box, an artificial nightingale which had been made to look like the live one, all set with diamonds, rubies and sapphires. When this artificial bird was wound up, it would sing one of the songs the live one sang and its tail would move up and down, all glittering with silver and gold. Round its neck hung a little band on which was written: "The nightingale of the Emperor of Japan is poor compared with the nightingale of the Emperor of China."

"How very charming!" they all exclaimed, and the person who had delivered the artificial bird was immediately given the title "Nightingale-Deliverer-in-Chief to his Imperial Majesty".

"Now they must sing together. What a duet that will make!"

And so they had to sing together but somehow it didn't seem right, for the artificial bird sang waltzes while the real nightingale sang in its natural style.

"You must not blame it for that," said the music master. "It's rhythm is faultless and is perfectly in keeping with the method advocated by my school."

So now the artificial bird was to sing alone. Its success was just as great as the real nightingale's and, besides, it was so much prettier to look at – it shone like a bracelet or a brooch.

Thirty-three times, over and over again, it sang the very same song without showing any sign of tiredness. They would have liked it to go on singing even more, but the Emperor said it was now the turn of the living nightingale to sing something. But where was she? Nobody had noticed her flying out through the open window, back to her own green wood.

"And how is this to be explained?" asked the Emperor. The courtiers were extremely annoyed and said the nightingale had behaved in a most ungrateful manner. "But still, we have the best bird," they said, and the artificial bird was made to sing yet again, making it the thirty-fourth time they had to listen to the same piece. But they still didn't know the song thoroughly because it was so difficult. The music master lavished extraordinary praise on the bird, declaring it was superior to the real nightingale not only in its plumage and the beauty of its diamonds but also because of its interior.

"For you see, my lords and ladies, and above all, Your

Imperial Majesty, with a real nightingale one can never tell what will come next but with the artificial bird everything takes place in a fixed arrangement. That is how it is and that is how it will stay! Everything in it can be demonstrated: one can open it up and show the human ingenuity behind it – where the waltzes are laid out, how they go and how one follows the other."

"That is precisely my opinion about it," they all said, and the music master was granted permission to show the bird to the people on the following Sunday: they too should hear it sing, commanded the Emperor. And hear it they did and they were as delighted as though they had got slightly drunk on tea (which, of course, is quite in accordance with what the Chinese do). And they all went, "Oh!" and "Ah!" and pointed their forefingers at it. But the poor fisherman, who had heard the real nightingale, said, "It sounds nice enough and it's not unlike the real thing, but there's something missing, I don't quite know what."

The real nightingale was banished from the Imperial realm.

The artificial bird had its place on a silken cushion near the Emperor's bed. All the gifts it had received, all the gold and precious stones, were arranged about it. Its title was now officially "High Imperial Night Singer" and in order of ranking it was advanced to Number One on the left hand side because the Emperor considered the side where the heart was to be the most important (and even in an Emperor that's the side where the heart is!). The music master wrote a work of twenty-five volumes about the artificial bird. It was very learned and very long, full of the most difficult words in the Chinese tongue. Yet everyone said they had read it and understood it, for otherwise they would have been considered stupid and had their stomachs trampled on.

Thus a whole year passed. The Emperor and the court and all the Chinese people knew by heart every single "cluck" in the artificial nightingale's song and they liked it all the more because of that: they could sing *with* it and this they did. The lads in the

street sang "zizizi" and "cluck-cluck-cluck" and even the
Emperor sang it. Yes, quite definitely, it was all most delightful.

But one evening, when the artificial bird was singing its best
and the Emperor was lying on his bed listening, there was a
sudden "trrrr-rrr-ppp" inside the bird, and a couple of seconds
later there was a distinct "crack!" You could hear the wheels
whirring round without being able to stop and then there was
silence. The music had stopped. The Emperor sprang out of bed
and summoned his personal physician. But what help could he
be? Then they sent for the watchmaker and after much talk and
investigation he managed to get the bird into some sort of
working order. But he warned that it should be used very
sparingly for the parts were getting very worn and you couldn't
really get replacements that would guarantee that the music
would continue as before. This was indeed a most sorry state of
affairs. From now on the bird was allowed to sing only once a
year and even that seemed to put a great strain on it. Then the
music master delivered a short speech with lots of difficult words,
the gist of which was that the bird was just as good as ever it was,
and so – what do you think? – it *was* as good as ever it was.

Five years went by and now the whole nation was plunged
into great sorrow for they were all very fond of their Emperor and
he was gravely ill and wasn't expected to live much longer.
Already a new Emperor had been chosen and the people stood
outside in the streets and asked the Court Cavalier how their
Emperor was getting on.

All he said was "P!" and shook his head.

Cold and pale the Emperor lay in his magnificent bed. The
court thought he was dead and each one ran to pay homage to
the new Emperor. The bedroom servants came out to have a
gossip about it and the ladies' maids held a coffee party. In the
corridors and passages cloth was laid down to soften people's
footsteps, and so everything was quiet, very quiet.

But the Emperor was not dead yet; stiff and white he lay on

his gorgeous bed with the long velvet hangings and the heavy gold tassels. High up, a window stood open and the moon shed its beams on the Emperor and the artificial bird.

The poor Emperor could hardly breathe; something seemed to be sitting on his chest. He opened his eyes . . . and he saw that it was Death sitting there and he had put on his golden crown and was holding in one hand the Emperor's golden sword and in the other his beautiful banner. And all around, from out of the folds of the great velvet hangings, strange heads thrust themselves out, some foul and ugly, others blessedly gentle. These were all the Emperor's good and bad deeds and now they were staring at him, as Death sat upon his chest.

"Do you remember this?" they whispered one after the other, and "Do you remember that?" Then they spoke to him of many things so that perspiration ran down the Emperor's brow.

"I have never known about that," said the Emperor. "Music! Music! The great drum of China!" he cried, "so that I may not hear what they are saying!"

But they went on talking and Death nodded like a Chinaman to everything they said.

"Music! Music!" cried the Emperor. "Precious golden bird, sing! Have I not given you gold and costly gifts? Have I not myself hung my golden slipper around your neck? Sing to me! Sing now!"

But the bird made not a sound. There was no one there to wind it. But Death continued to stare at the Emperor from his great empty eye-sockets and all was still and silent, fearfully silent.

Then, quite suddenly, from somewhere very close to the window, there burst forth the most glorious song. It was the little nightingale sitting outside on a bough. She had heard about the Emperor's distress and had come to sing to him to give him comfort and hope. And as she sang the shadowy forms round the Emperor grew fainter and fainter, the blood coursed quicker and quicker through the Emperor's weak body and even Death listened and said, "Keep singing, little nightingale, keep singing!"

"But will you give me the royal gold sword, the rich banner and the Emperor's crown?"

And Death surrendered all these treasures in return for a song. And the nightingale sang on and on. She sang of the quiet churchyard where the white roses grow, where the elder tree smells sweet and the cool grass is moistened by the tears of the bereaved. And then Death yearned for his garden and he floated, like a cold white mist, out through the open window.

"Thank you, thank you!" said the Emperor. "Divine little bird! I know you well. I sent you away from my land and my empire and yet you have sung away the evil visions from my bed and lifted Death from my heart. How can I repay you?"

"You have repaid me!" replied the nightingale. "I drew tears from your eyes when I sang to you the first time, and that I shall never forget. Those tears were jewels that rejoice the heart of the singer. But now you must sleep and awake fresh and strong once more. I shall sing to you."

And she sang, and the Emperor sank into a sweet sleep. How soothing and refreshing that sleep was! The sun shone upon him through the windows and when he awoke, strengthened and restored, not one of his servants had yet come back to see him, for they all thought he was dead. But the nightingale still sat beside him and sang.

"Stay with me always," said the Emperor. "You shall sing only when it pleases you, and the artificial bird I shall break into a thousand pieces."

"No, don't do that," said the nightingale, "it has done its best. Keep it as you have done before. But I cannot build my nest in the palace and live here. Let me come here when I wish. Then, in the evenings, I shall sit on a bough near the window and sing for you so that you may think about happy things. I shall sing of those who are fortunate and of those who suffer. I shall sing of the good and evil that is hidden round about you. The little singing bird flies far and wide: to the poor fisherman, to the farmer's thatched cottage, to all those who dwell far from you and your court. I love your heart more dearly than your crown, even though your crown is itself sacred. I shall come and I shall sing to you, but one thing you must promise me."

"I will promise anything you ask," said the Emperor, standing now in his royal robes, which he had put on himself, and holding to his heart his sword heavy with gold.

"One thing I ask you: Tell no one that you have a little bird who tells you everything . . ."

And the nightingale flew away.

The servants came in to see their dead Emperor, but lo! there he stood!

And the Emperor said, "Good morning!"